Shimmy

Shimmy

Kari Jones

PAPL
DISCARDED

ORCA BOOK PUBLISHERS

Copyright © 2015 Kari Jones

All rights reserved. No part of this publication may be reproduced or transmitted in any form or by any means, electronic or mechanical, including photocopying, recording or by any information storage and retrieval system now known or to be invented, without permission in writing from the publisher.

Library and Archives Canada Cataloguing in Publication

Jones, Kari, 1966–, author
Shimmy / Kari Jones.
(Orca limelights)

Issued in print and electronic formats.
ISBN 978-1-4598-0764-8 (pbk.).—ISBN 978-1-4598-0765-5 (pdf).—
ISBN 978-1-4598-0766-2 (epub)

I. Title. II. Series: Orca limelights
PS8619.O5328S55 2015   jC813'.6   C2015-901700-9
C2015-901701-7

First published in the United States, 2015
Library of Congress Control Number: 2015935512

Summary: In this short novel for middle readers, a famous belly dancer invites Lila to join her prestigious studio, and Lila must decide whether to leave the dance teacher and troupe she loves.

MIX
Paper from
responsible sources
FSC
www.fsc.org   FSC® C103214

Cover design by Rachel Page
Cover photography by iStockphoto.com

ORCA BOOK PUBLISHERS
www.orcabook.com

Printed and bound in Canada.

18   17   16   15   •   4   3   2   1

*To Goldean and Candace and all the dancers,
and in memory of Angela.*

One

"Ooh la la," I say as Amala holds a silky turquoise mermaid skirt up to her waist. The girls in the dance troupe laugh.

"Exactly. We'll wear them at the festival, with mirrored hip scarves over them and colored lace tops. You girls will look so elegant!" Amala smiles broadly as she speaks, and the girls in the room shimmer with happiness. She lifts an orange hip scarf from a pile at her feet and wraps it around the skirt. Fingernail-sized mirrors in the scarf sparkle in the lights.

"It's awesome," Angela says. She takes the skirt and scarf from Amala, holds them to her body and twirls. The panels flare out around her feet, and the rest of us clap.

"Let's go through the choreography one more time, and then we'll break for the day," Amala says. "Try the skirt on for size sometime during the week and decide on a color, and I'll put in the orders on Friday."

We strike our starting pose: arms up, palms facing out, head down and away from the audience, body turned slightly to the left. I glance at Angela behind me and roll my shoulders back and down. She copies me, and her posture straightens. I nod and settle back into pose.

Amala moves the pile of scarves and the skirt to the side of the studio and takes her place in front of us. She presses the remote, and the drums start.

We hold the pose for eight beats, then turn slowly, snaking our arms around our bodies so we make a wave of motion on the stage. The music gathers speed as the violin and cello sing out a rhythm over the beat of the drums, and we slip into a traveling step layered with hip shimmies and chest lifts. With a roll of drums, we twirl. Oh, I can already imagine the burst of color a line of girls in mermaid skirts and mirrored scarves will make when we're crossing the stage.

The accordion picks up the melody, and we follow along with some classic belly-dance moves. I'm grinning, because I can see how the mirrored scarves are going to sparkle as we drop our right hips and kick, and the lace tops will show off our chest circles.

We all gather in pairs, and Angela and I dance into the center of the room. This is the part I love, when Angela and I dance next to each other. The music takes over as all the instruments fall into one melody, and it becomes one with my body. The scarf mirrors are going to dazzle the audience during this sequence of slow turns and undulations, and the skirts will swirl around us. The audience will go crazy. We'll be the stars of the show. It'll be my first step on the way to becoming a professional belly dancer.

There's a pause of one count in the music, and I close my eyes to feel it, then raise my arms above my head and sink into a hip drop. The music builds from slow to fast, and we pick up a shimmy starting at our hips and working up to our shoulders so that our bodies quiver.

The sound of the violin fills the room, and our arms catch the mood and snake around our bodies again for a count of eight. Energy radiates from our fingertips as we swirl one last time, lift our arms and finish.

My fingers tingle, and I whirl around and pull Angela into a hug.

"Well done, girls. We're getting there," Amala says. She opens the studio door, and early spring air from the lobby wafts in. We all head to the edges of the studio for our water bottles, which Angela and I always leave by the door so we can be the first ones into the lobby after class. Everyone is laughing and smiling at each other. That was a great class.

"You looked fantastic, as always," I say to Angela.

"I felt okay, but I still want to work on that sequence with the hips. I get the right half of the figure eight, but my left hip never wants to do it properly," Angela says.

She's wearing a blue tank top and deep-purple pants with a gathered fringe around her ankles. With her long dark hair and thick eyelashes, she looks like a belly dancer even without costume or makeup.

Angela and I have been friends since our moms signed us up for dance classes at the Oak Bay rec center when we were five. We've been dancing together for ten years now, and we've been BFFS all that time, so I know that even though Angela did the whole dance absolutely perfectly, she'll work on her moves and correct herself until the moment we walk onstage. Angela loves to dance, but performances make her nervous.

"You were perfect." I take a swig from my water bottle and head to my cubbyhole for my shoes and coat. I never take Angela's doubts too seriously. She'll be fantastic once she gets onto the stage.

She shrugs and shakes herself from head to toe. "We'll see."

"The festival's going to be amazing. We're going to be fantastic. Everything's going to be awesome!" I say. The spirit of the dance is still in me, and it makes me jump around the room. Nini and Sarit laugh beside me.

"You're really looking forward to the festival, aren't you?" Sarit says.

"I am." There's no use pretending—I've wanted to be a professional dancer for at least the past three years, and they all know it. This is the first festival we've been invited to, and it makes me feel like shouting with happiness.

"Let's go before we miss the bus," Angela says.

Girls are packing up around us, and Angela and I pull on our shoes and coats, but before we're finished, Amala comes into the doorway and says, "One last thing, girls. I have a surprise for you." She takes a deep breath. "Dana Sajala has asked me to choose three girls from my classes to join her studio."

The lobby goes silent. We stand frozen, water bottles partway to our lips, shoes half pulled onto our feet, coats hanging off our arms, as the news sinks in. Then Sarit says, "Dana Sajala?" and the spell is broken. My heart pounds so loudly I can hear it in my ears.

"You mean to perform with her troupe for the festival?" Nini asks.

"Yes—and continue on as one of her students." Amala's smile is super wide, because she knows the opportunity she's offering. Dana Sajala is one of the best-known belly dancers in the world. A chance to dance with her would be the perfect start to any career.

"Who have you chosen?" Nini asks. It's what we all want to know, and I can almost feel everyone sucking in their breath.

6

"I haven't yet. I'll tell you next week." Amala holds up her hands and laughs as the noise level rises. "No, don't ask me now. I'm not saying anything more until I've spoken to Dana and made my final decision."

When Amala heads back into the studio, leaving us girls alone, it takes a minute before we start moving again. The fabric of my coat brushes roughly against my arms, and my feet feel squished in my Toms. There's murmuring all around me, and Sarit says something to Angela as we walk out the door, but I don't hear what it is, because a voice in my head is shouting, *Dana Sajala! Dana Sajala!*

It's a chance of a lifetime!

Two

"She has to choose us!" I say to Angela as we wait for the bus home. The tangy ocean air fills me with energy, and since the music from class is still in my mind, I bust out a few hip circles in time to the beat. Two boys standing behind us laugh. Angela glances back at the boys and shuffles her feet.

"Ignore them. Dana Sajala is taking on students, and we are going to be two of them!" I grab Angela's hands and swing her around, but she resists and pulls her hands away. "What?" I ask.

Before Angela can respond, a bunch of kids from a nearby school's basketball team crowd into the bus shelter. Then the bus pulls up, and we all jostle on. I head for a free seat, but there is an old lady behind me, so I step aside and give it to her. The aisle is crowded, and somehow Angela ends up halfway down the bus from me. The basketball kids call to one another along the aisle, and one at the back says something that makes all of them laugh. It's infectious, and I laugh with them, though I don't know what's funny. I'm just happy, that's all.

The driver pulls into the road, and we make our slow way down the hill toward home. The bus route takes us along the ocean, where the sound of the waves mingles with the laughter and chatter bubbling around me, and it's easy to slip into daydreaming. I can see it now: we're onstage in the signature costume of Dana's studio—multi-tiered ruffle skirts in bright colors, with tassel belts and matching midriff tops called cholis. The music starts, and we begin our dance. We are like birds flocking, each girl so in tune with the others that we look like one being. Our movements are graceful, and our timing is perfect. Dana watches, and as we twirl around to the front, she catches my eye and smiles, and I know she's seen me. *Me*. When the music ends and we walk off the stage, she pulls me over and says, "I'm glad

Amala chose you to come to me. You're going to be one of my star students." A shiver tingles down my spine.

The bus stops and a bunch of kids get off. It's rush hour, and the lights and noise of downtown Victoria jolt me out of my dream. At the far end of the bus Angela is staring into space, a frown on her face. There's something about her mouth and the way her body sags a bit into the seat next to her that makes me wonder if she's upset.

As we near our stop, I push my way down the aisle until I'm standing next to Angela. The bus hits a bump and jostles us, and she says, "There you are."

"You okay?" I ask.

"Of course."

"Sure?"

Angela smiles and flips her hair over her shoulder like she does when she's happy. The bus pulls up at our stop, and Angela and I push past the basketball players to the door and step off. In the sudden quiet of our neighborhood, Angela and I shimmy our way down the sidewalk. We swing around cherry trees, shaking them as we pass so their pink and white petals spray over us.

"Amala's going to choose us," I say. "She has to—we're the best dancers in the whole class. By far."

Angela laughs and rolls her shimmy up her whole body.

"I can't believe we're going to dance with Dana Sajala. Can you believe it?" I say.

Angela stops shimmying and says, "She might not choose us. You do know that, right?"

"Spoilsport!" I say. The wind has blown cherry petals across the path and into the spruce hedge in front of Angela's house so that it looks like a dancer's colorful skirt. I pull some of the petals off and put them in my hair for decoration.

"Let me dream my dream," I say as Angela turns into her yard.

"Amala has a whole studio to choose from, Lila. She might not choose you. Or me. Or anyone else from our class."

"But she will," I say.

"Just..." She hesitates.

"Just what?"

Angela shifts her bag on her shoulder and doesn't say anything for a few moments, but when she sees I'm about to ask her again, she says,

"Don't persuade yourself Amala's going to choose us, that's all."

"Why not?" I ask.

"Because I don't want you to be disappointed. I know you," she says. "You always believe things are going to happen." With that she walks up the path and onto the stairs in front of her house.

"But…" I don't know what to say, so I watch her fit the key into the lock of her door. As she opens it, I say, "Don't you think Amala could choose us?"

"She might. But she might not."

"You think there are others in the class who are better than us?" It seems unlikely.

"I don't know. I just don't want you to get super excited about something that might not happen." Angela turns the knob, enters her house and leaves me standing on the walkway, wondering, Is there someone more likely to be chosen?

Doubt gnaws at my stomach, making me feel sick. I really, really, *really* want to be chosen. But what if I'm not?

Three

"Girls, let's show Dana our best," says Amala as she opens the door and lets Dana into the room. We've been drilling the choreography, and now Dana is here to watch us dance. I can hardly stand it. I've been waiting for this moment for seven whole days—ever since last week's class.

"Hello, girls," Dana says. Her skirt swirls around her knees, and her long hair shines. We all straighten our posture as she joins Amala at the front of the room.

"Ready?" Amala asks. We settle into our pose. I can feel Dana's eyes on me. I take a deep breath and exhale slowly. Amala presses the remote and we start.

I love this music, and I love the way Amala's choreography picks up the trills of the drum, the thick, sticky line of the cello and violin, and the quick movements of the accordion. We start with our chest lifts and hip circles, accenting the bass with our hips and the treble with our arms. As I dance, my mind drifts to what Dana must be seeing and thinking, and my body suddenly feels like lead. My arms stutter instead of flow, and my hips miss the beat. When it comes time to move into pairs, my feet drag, and when Nini bumps into me, I stop.

"Ouch," I say and rub my shin.

"We'll start again from the beginning," says Amala.

"Can we get a sip of water first?" says Nini, and before Amala can answer, everyone scurries to the edges of the room.

"What's wrong?" Angela asks.

I shrug and take a sip of water so I don't have to answer, but I know what's wrong. Doubt is kicking at me, making me clumsy. All through the class I've been glancing around at the other girls. Nini is so elegant, and Sarit bursts with energy. Ellen, Flora, Petra—they're all so quick and supple. Any one of them could get picked. It's making me panic. What if Amala *doesn't* choose Angela and me?

"Dana is making me nervous," says Angela.

She's right. That's all it is. Nerves.

"I wish Amala would tell us already, so we didn't have to do all this," I say.

"I guess she wants Dana to see her picks in action." She smiles and tosses her hair over her shoulder.

"Do you know something?" I ask.

"Of course not," she says, and she replaces her water bottle on the ledge and heads back to her spot. She doesn't appear nervous. As always, she looks perfect.

"Again," says Amala, and in the second before the music starts I sneak a glance at Dana, who catches my eye and smiles at me. My heart leaps into the first drum beat, and the lead falls away from my body.

The music continues, and from the corner of my eye I can see that our lines are straight, and our posture is strong. We are all smiling.

The music ends, and Amala presses the remote. "The girls look good, don't they, Dana?"

"I love your choreography, Amala. You've caught the music beautifully," Dana says as she weaves between us on a tour of the room. "And you're right," she adds when she reaches Amala's side again. "I approve of your choice of student."

We all gasp. Like one big guppy, we suck in our cheeks and turn to Amala.

Amala frowns. "I was going to wait until class was over, but okay. I'll tell you now." She pauses, and her eyes travel across the room until they meet mine. "Lila, would you like to join Dana's studio as one of her students?"

My body explodes. Everything from my fingertips to my toes to the ends of my hair tingles. I can barely even nod, I'm bursting so much, but I still hold my breath because I'm waiting for Amala's eyes to continue their sweep of the room and land on Angela. But they don't. Instead, they swivel back to Dana, who smiles at me.

"Who are the other two girls you've chosen?" Nini asks.

"Laura and Savana from my Thursday-evening class," says Amala.

The tingle fades as I realize it's only me going, not me and Angela. It's hard to know where to look. I want to see Angela's face, but I also don't want to. But then Angela shoves through Flora and Nini and scoops me up in a bear hug, which Sarit and Petra join her in, and soon the whole room rushes me in a big scrum. My body finally stops tingling, and I let out my breath. I catch Amala's eye across the room, and she smiles at me and nods. I smile back.

The other girls let go, but Angela keeps hugging me, so finally I pull back so I can see her properly. Her whole face smiles, including her eyes.

"I wish you were coming," I whisper into her ear.

She shakes her head. "You deserve it," she says, and with those words the whole thing hits me.

I'm going to dance with one of the troupes in Dana Sajala's studio!

"Don't forget us, please," says Flora, which makes everyone laugh.

"I won't," I promise.

Angela finally lets me go, and I make my way back to my spot, but Amala says, "Lila, I think we'd better practice without you so the girls can get used to not having anyone in that space. You can sit and watch." She motions to the side of the room.

Of course. I'm not dancing this dance anymore. It's beautiful choreography, though, and I have to admit to feeling a pang when I sit down next to the wall to watch the troupe practice.

The dance is gorgeous. The girls know the music well, and they move together gracefully. Even having eleven girls onstage instead of twelve works, because instead of going into pairs, Amala directs them into clumps of three and four. I'm sad to leave, but I'm going on to something even more exciting. I only wish Angela was coming, and I hope she's not too disappointed.

The force of what's happened hits me again, and the tingling in my fingers returns.

I've been chosen to dance for Dana Sajala.

It's going to be fantastic.

Four

English class is never going to end. Mrs. O'Connor drones on about *To Kill a Mockingbird*. This lesson should be called *To Kill the Reading Experience*. I hardly slept at all last night, what with the excitement and nervousness of being chosen to dance for Dana, and now it's all I can do to stay awake for twelve more minutes. When Mrs. O'Connor finally stops talking and the bell rings, I'm so close to sleep that I have to shake out my arms and legs before I can get up. It takes me a few minutes to gather my books and pens and cram them into my backpack and head out the door.

"There you are," Angela says when I reach the courtyard behind the auditorium. She and Nini and Sarit are already sitting at one of the picnic tables set up among the garden beds. Angela has been working in the veggie gardens all year for her service hours, and we often come here at lunchtime so she can weed after we eat. I had been hoping to find Angela alone, but I guess that's not going to happen.

"Congratulations," Nini says to me.

"Thanks," I say.

"I bet it's going to be amazing," Sarit says.

"Yeah. I hope so," I say. It's too warm in my sweater, so I take it off and throw it across the table. The sun feels soft on my arms.

"What are you eating?" Sarit asks as I pull my lunch out of my backpack.

"Mom made me a smoothie with raspberries and yogurt and orange juice in it, and a bowl of quinoa and spinach. She was so cute when she gave it to me. Feeding me for success, she said."

"Your mom's so nice," Nini says.

"She's pretty proud of me," I say.

"I wish Dana would pick me. Then maybe my mom would make me smoothies and salads, and I wouldn't have to make stupid ham sandwiches," Nini says.

"Yeah. The only thing is..." I stop because suddenly I'm embarrassed.

"The only thing is what?" Nini asks.

"It's a lot to live up to. Part of me wants to stay with Amala. I'm pretty nervous."

"Says the girl who wants to be a professional dancer." Nini unwraps her sandwich and takes a big bite.

"It's a big step," I say.

"I hear Dana's really picky. My sister's friend danced with her last year, and she said one time Dana kept them for an extra hour until they got the timing right in one of their sequences," Sarit says.

"That's the kind of thing that's making me anxious," I say.

Sarit's voice is gentle. "I thought it was exactly what you wanted."

"Yeah, I know. It is. I'm totally excited, but it's also giving me a stomachache."

Nini leans forward so she's chewing her sandwich right in front of my face. "Dancing with Dana is something we'd all like to do. You're getting the chance of a lifetime, so buck up, girl. I don't want to hear anything more about nervousness."

Nini and I are good friends, and being direct like this is just her way, but there's a hint of jealousy in Nini's voice that makes my smoothie feel thick in my throat.

She leans back, takes another bite of her sandwich and chews it loudly. No one says anything more about dancing while we finish our lunches.

When she's done eating, Nini stands up and slings her backpack over her shoulder. "I need to go meet Mrs. O'Connor. She said she'd help me with my English essay," she says.

"I'll come with you," says Sarit.

Angela and I sit at the table and watch them walk across the courtyard. "It *would* be a lot easier for me to go if you were coming too," I say.

"Amala chose you, Lila."

"But I wish she had chosen you too." Instead of finishing my quinoa, I toss it into the compost.

Angela frowns at me and says, "No grains in the compost—you know that. It brings rats."

It's true. We had an announcement about it last week. With a sigh, I pick what I can of the quinoa out of the compost and put it back in my container. "I had dreams of us dancing together at the festival," I say.

22

"Well, you don't have to go to Dana's studio," Angela says.

"I know."

"Seriously, you don't."

"You want me to stay with Amala?" I ask. The quinoa rolls around in my stomach, making it hurt even more.

"You always said you loved Amala's choreography and the music," Angela says. "If you really want to dance with me, you don't have to go to Dana's studio. It's your choice—that's all I'm saying."

Is she serious? "You want me to give up an opportunity of a lifetime?" I ask.

"That's not what I meant."

Strangely, though two seconds ago I was feeling nervous about going to Dana's studio, now that Angela has said I don't have to go, I know I really want to.

"I know. But yes, I do want to go do Dana's. I do. As Nini says, it's a great opportunity, but I wish you were coming too!"

"I'm totally happy at Amala's," Angela says.

"What's that supposed to mean?" I ask.

She shrugs. "Not everyone wants to dance with Dana, Lila."

It's the first I've heard of this. "Don't you want to be a professional? Don't you think dancing with Dana is a fantastic opportunity?" I ask.

"For sure. For you. Just not what I want, that's all." She takes the last bite of her apple and tosses the core into the compost, then packs up her lunch and pulls her gardening gloves out of her backpack. "I need to weed out the winter spinach. Want to help?"

I shake my head and watch her cross the courtyard. Angela is one of the most beautiful dancers I've ever seen. I'm almost surprised Dana picked me over her. How can she not want to dance with Dana? It doesn't make any sense. No sense at all.

Five

By the time I board the bus to Dana Sajala's studio after school, I feel like I might throw up at any moment. I show the bus driver my pass and head for a seat at the back, where a pile of noisy basketball players are laughing and tossing around someone's phone. My coat is too warm for this spring day, but there's not enough room to take it off, and I end up with it bunched around my waist, making me even hotter. The basketball players keep tossing the phone between them, and I try to concentrate on its path through the air, but that does nothing to make the nervousness go away.

When my stop comes at last, I scramble to gather my coat and bags and only manage to lurch off the bus at the last second. The studio is downtown, and there are so many people walking along the sidewalk that it takes me a few minutes to find the right door, which turns out to be hidden behind a huge sandwich board for a coffee shop next door. My breath comes fast as I step into the lobby.

There's no one here. Just a cupboard at the end of the room and a small table with white lilies in a glass vase. The air is still and cool. I almost expect to hear soothing music coming from hidden speakers. It seems I've stepped into a lawyer's office, not the foyer of a dance studio. Before I can decide I've really walked into the wrong spot, Dana opens another door and sees me.

"Lila, great to see you. Come in, come in. The girls are waiting for you." Dana's presence in the room changes everything. The air around her vibrates, and suddenly the room seems warm. She strides over to the cupboard and opens it; a trail of perfume follows her. I stare after her until she says, "Hang up your coat and take a second to settle, then join us in the studio."

I hang my coat up and take a moment to straighten my clothes. I've dreamed of this moment.

I wipe my palms on my pants, roll my shoulders back and step into the studio like a dancer, just as Amala taught us. Dana smiles at me as I pass her, and I grow an inch or two.

The studio is much like Amala's, with mirrors on both sides of the room and a springy wooden floor to dance on. But at the far end, where the computer and speakers are set up, is a shelf where hip scarves are arranged by color and a rail where a row of matching ruffle skirts hangs. Below them is a series of wicker boxes labeled *black, white, purple, pink, turquoise* and *gold*. None of the piles of rumpled scarves and skirts that always lie around at Amala's studio.

The troupe of girls is totally different too. Everyone in this group looks like a professional dancer. I never really noticed it before, but that's not true at Amala's studio. Some of the girls at Amala's studio are not very fit. But in Dana's troupe, everyone is slim and stands with excellent posture. They look like the dancers you see on TV. Instinctively, I roll my shoulders back again.

"This is Lila. She'll be dancing with us over the next weeks as we get ready for the festival," says Dana.

The girls break formation and crowd around me.

"We wondered who was coming," says a tall girl with long dark hair, in a pink T-shirt and the kind of pants Angela always dances in.

Another girl pushes through the others until she's standing next to me. She is wearing black yoga pants and a turquoise tank top that shows off her muscular arms. "You're going to love it here," she says.

There's a murmur in the crowd, and someone else says, "We all love it here."

"I'm sure I will," I say, and as I say those words I really mean them. I've only been here for five minutes, but everything is as I imagined it. The girls are perfect. The studio is wonderful. Professionalism oozes from every part of it, even the foyer with its white lilies.

Dana says, "Girls, let's do a few drills to warm up and to show Lila what it's like around here. There are only a few weeks before the festival, so the pressure's on."

The girls scurry back to their places, and I find a spot at the end of the back row.

"Lila, we always start with our posture, as I'm sure Amala has taught you. Feet firmly planted, knees slightly bent, pelvis rolled gently forward, ribs open, shoulders back, arms in second position and chin tucked slightly in toward the chest." The girls shuffle and settle into position, and Dana turns on the music. "Hips downbeat left, moving to the right," she says as she leads us into the drill.

It's different from what I'm used to, but I like it, and it's easy to follow the count as we start a series of quarter-time hip circles. Dana turns around and watches us. I follow her eyes as she takes in each of us, and as I do, the nervous knot inside me eases. Every girl has the movement down perfectly. No shoulders sway; no heads bob. Dana catches my eye and smiles at me, and the last of my case of nerves vanishes.

This is going to be fantastic.

"Lila, we're going to run through the choreography for the festival. I'll call out the pattern as we go. Follow along as best you can," says Dana.

I take a deep breath and nod. Dana starts the music, and the girls spring into action. The choreography is daring and fun. It starts with three girls grouped at stage right. They do a short sequence of hip twists and arm lifts, then step back in a triplet so their bodies mimic the bounce of the drum beat. On the next beat, the three girls to their left pick up an undulation that starts in their hips and rises to their shoulders, following the guitar-like strums of the oud. They circle each other and pass the movement over to the next batch of girls, who flutter their arms around their bodies along with the notes of the oboe. The effect is of a carnival of motion passing across the stage.

I'm in the next group. Dana calls out her instructions for us. "Figure eight starting on the left hip, swing around to face center, right shoulder forward, then back."

I stumble through the moves, slightly offbeat, my face red as I notice every girl in the room watching, but Dana smiles at me, so I keep going until my little group joins the rest of the dancers in the chorus and no one pays attention to me anymore. *I can do this!*

The drums pick up speed, and the oud starts a conversation with the oboe that grows louder and louder while we twirl and shimmy and kick across the stage, each clump of girls following a different instrument. By the end I am breathless.

"Got it?" Dana asks when the song finishes.

I'm surprised by the question, since Amala never assumes we'll learn a choreography in one go, but Dana looks at me expectantly, so I nod my head yes and hope it's true.

"Good. We'll go through it again. This time, Lila, focus on your posture. I noticed a bit of shoulder hunching last run-through."

I soften my knees and shake out the tension in my neck before I say, "Okay."

At the end of class, Dana says, "Work on that timing, girls" as we file out of the room. I try to catch her eye as I pass her, but she's talking to another girl and doesn't notice me.

In the lobby, the tall girl who spoke first earlier says, "Well done, Lila. We weren't sure if you'd be able to keep up, but you did great."

Everything in me swells, and I feel like I could float away.

Six

"How was it?" are the first words out of Angela's mouth the next morning on the bus to school.

I sigh. "It was perfect. Dana's so professional, and she really watches the dancers. She corrects even the smallest faults in posture and timing. It's...it's like we're professionals. Dana doesn't let us get away with anything."

"Well, that's good," she says.

"And wait till you see the dance, and the girls—they all *look* like dancers, you know? It's more than how they dress or how well they dance. It's in the way they stand, the way they *are*. It's so amazing to be there. Our performance is going to blow everyone else out of the water."

"Oh," says Angela with a frown.

"Don't get me wrong," I say. "Amala's choreography is good. You guys are going to do great."

"Good? Two days ago you loved it," she says.

"Yeah, but then I saw Dana's. Her choreography is really fantastic. It's cheeky—you know, fun. It's like she's really listened to the music and heard it. The choreography catches everything, and each girl shows off a different part of the music."

"You sure know a lot after one class," Angela says. The bus pulls to a stop and Sarit and Nini get on.

"Yeah, I know. I learned more from her in one day..." I say to Angela, and I'm about to tell her that Dana taught me to start a shimmy in my thighs rather than in my knees so it's easier to walk with it, but Nini plunks down behind us, leans over the seat and says, "So the new boy, Jonas—I talked to him after school yesterday."

"Really?" says Angela. She swivels around in her seat so she's facing Nini and Sarit. "Tell me everything, Nini." It's like she's cut me off. Like she didn't want to hear any more.

"He's so nice. Turns out he lives down the street from me, and he actually carried my books home. Imagine. It was so old-fashioned, but in a good way," Nini says.

"You're in love with him!" Sarit says, shoving Nini in the arm.

"Am not," she says, but she blushes madly as she says it, so we all laugh.

"He has a sister named Beatrix. I met her too. She dances with Dana, by the way, Lila. Maybe she's in your class. She's tall and blond, and she looks a lot like Jonas. Hey, how was your first class?" Nini asks.

"Give us details," Angela says to Nini before I can answer. "What did he say?"

Nini leans back in her seat and says, "He asked me if I always catch that bus home."

Sarit giggles and says, "He so likes you!"

"I think I met his sister yesterday at Dana's studio," I say. "Dana has this amazing part of her choreography where we all come in together like a pinwheel, and Bea stands next to me in that formation. Dana says the choreography of any dance should have different formations to keep the audience's attention."

"Wait," says Angela. "How did you meet Beatrix?"

"She was in the class," I say.

"I was talking to Nini," she says.

It's like in dance when you miss a beat, and everything that comes after is wrong. Nini tells us all about how Jonas invited her into his house and made her a cup of tea, which is where she met Beatrix, and of course I want to hear what she says, but by the time we get off the bus, we've heard all about Nini's visit with Jonas, but they haven't heard anything at all about Dana's class, and as we head into school, they don't even ask.

* * *

It's easier walking into the studio this afternoon now that I know where to go, but I'm still nervous because although I drilled the choreography every lunchtime and evening since last week's class, I still don't know it super well. My bus from school arrives only a couple of minutes before class starts, so the girls are already in the studio when I get there, and I have to pull off my shoes and coat quickly and run into the room.

"Drills again today, girls. I want to get the timing and sequencing of the drum section down," says Dana as she strides into the room. We each find our spot in the room and settle into the starting posture. Dana starts the music, and we dance. The opening sequence goes well, and our timing is perfect as we pass the movement from one group of girls to the next.

"Good," says Dana.

We start the next sequence, where the whole troupe shimmies into the center and creates a pinwheel. The timing's tricky here, and I'm out of step by one beat.

Dana pauses the music. "Lila, let's go over the transition into the center. It's right foot behind left, twirl, and step out left so you're balanced for the shimmy starting on your right." I nod, but she motions to me to try it, so I go through the sequence as she's described it. She frowns and stands beside me.

"Do it with me," she says. We move together, right foot behind, twirl, step out left. At that point she puts her hand on my shoulder and says, "Step out a tiny bit more; that will balance you better. There you go." And she's right. It does feel better.

"Got it?" she asks.

"Got it."

Dana returns to the front of the room, and we pick up where we left off. This time the transition is smooth, and we all enter the pinwheel formation on time.

"Good," Dana calls.

The music continues, and we circle around each other, creating a wave of motion clockwise and then counterclockwise. We drill it again, but this time as we turn around the circle, Bea and I bump right into each other.

Dana stops the music. "Girls, break for a minute," she says. "Get yourselves some water while I work with Bea on this."

We walk to the edges of the room for our water bottles. I reach for mine past the tall girl with long dark hair, who rolls her eyes and says, "Bea never gets transitions." There's something brittle about how she stands, but it takes me a second to realize she's pissed off.

I take a sip of water, then say, "I hope we're not stopped for long."

"I know, right?" she says, rolling her eyes again.

A red-haired girl joins us and says, "Chill, Eve. It'll all be better when we're on that stage and everyone's perfect."

Eve nods and shakes out her shoulders and neck. "Yep, you're right." She smiles at me and walks back to the center of the room.

"Eve takes her dance time very seriously, but don't worry—she's as critical of herself," the redhead says. "I'm Sam, by the way."

I keep an eye on Eve as we go back into our practice. She's good. Her movements are effortless and graceful, and her body control is stunning. It's hard to isolate a particular part of the body so that only one muscle group is moving, but when Eve does shoulder lifts, only her shoulders lift. When she does hip drops, only her hips drop. I can't see that there's much to be critical about. She's the best dancer in the class for sure. Someone to watch and learn from.

Dana stands next to Bea through the next two drills and calls out every move she makes, and I also watch closely. I didn't say anything to Eve or Sam, but deep down I am afraid it might have been me who was out of step when we bumped, not Bea.

Seven

In the evening, I practice the choreography over and over, until I know it by heart and could dance it in my sleep. In fact, I do dance it in my sleep—at least, that's what it feels like, because I dream the steps all night long, and when I wake up, I'm tired and my body's sore. I'm slow to get going in the morning, and I miss the first bus, so it's only when I slide into my seat in English that I finally see Angela.

I have news, Angela writes in the margin of her notebook.

I lean over the table and write back, *Tell.*

It's about Jonas!!! she writes.

The exclamation marks say everything. I start to write back, but Mrs. O'Connor asks the class to compose a short paragraph on whether or not it really is a sin to kill a mockingbird, and Angela pulls her notebook back to her side of the desk. Sigh. That's so not the point of the book. Doesn't Mrs. O'Connor know that?

When English class is over, Angela and I head to the courtyard for our lunch. I should be doing the homework that I skipped last night, but Angela pulls on my arm and steers me out of the class. "I have to talk to you," she says as we push through the door.

We barely reach the picnic table before Angela plunks her lunch down and says, "Jonas asked me out."

"What? When?" I say. So much for eating lunch. This is news.

"Next Wednesday evening. He wants to take me to a movie."

"What about Nini?" I ask.

"Exactly. Promise you won't tell. Promise?"

"But I thought Nini was in love with him," I say.

"She is, but..." Angela seems to find her lunch box super interesting suddenly. She picks it up and stares at it from every angle. When she looks up, she says, "I *really* like him."

"Wait. Wednesday you have dance," I say.

"I know. I'll have to miss the class."

"You're going to miss dance class to go out with a boy you hardly even know?"

"People do it," Angela says.

"Good thing you aren't dancing with Dana. She'd never let you get away with that," I say.

"Good thing."

"Actually, Dana says we should be dancing every day. Oh, she told me a new way to do chest lifts that I want to show you. It'll help you with that sequence you've been having trouble with. Look." It's easier to show dance moves standing up, so I get up from the table and settle myself into a dance posture so that I can show Angela how chest lifts are way easier if you constrict the muscles in your upper back between your shoulder blades.

"I said I really like him, Lila," Angela says. "Aren't you listening? I *really* like him."

"Really like who?" says Nini. She and Sarit slide onto the picnic bench and pull out their lunches. We do this every day. It's not like Angela didn't know they were coming. Angela stares at me with a look that says, *Keep quiet!*

"The new puppy she wants her dad to get her," I say. Well, it is true, even if it's not the truth she happened to be talking about right now.

"Guess what? I invited Jonas and Bea to join us for lunch," Nini says. Both she and Sarit giggle, and Angela widens her eyes and stares at me even harder. Before I can say or do anything, Jonas and Bea walk across the courtyard.

"I need to do some weeding," says Angela when they join us. She gets up from the table and packs away her lunch. I notice she hasn't looked directly at Jonas at all, but her face is redder than usual.

"I'll help," says Jonas, and when Sarit and Nini both turn to stare at him, he adds, "I need volunteer hours."

"Your brother's so nice," Nini says to Bea as Angela and Jonas head to the garden beds. The ones farthest away, I can't help but notice.

Bea shrugs.

"I was showing Angela what Dana told us yesterday about using your upper back muscles for chest lifts," I say to Sarit and Nini. "Want to see?"

"I feel a sudden urge to weed," Sarit says, and she and Nini giggle.

"Angela says those ones over there need work," I say, pointing to a bed in the corner of the courtyard opposite Angela and Jonas.

"Ha-ha," says Nini. She pulls Sarit up by the arm, and the two of them march off to the bed where Angela and Jonas are working. I don't know which one I should feel sorry for, Angela for being interrupted, or Nini for not getting that Jonas would rather be with Angela than with her.

"I hope you don't mind that I asked Alex and Robin to join us," Bea says as two girls come into the courtyard. It's getting to be like Grand Central Station around here, but I recognize Alex and Robin from Dana's class, so I'm happy to see them.

"Hey," I say as they sit down, and soon the four of us are deep in a conversation about the intricacies of Dana's choreography and how beautiful it is.

"She always uses the music so well," says Alex.

"I love the beginning sequence of our dance, the way the movement washes across the stage and how we all end up in a pinwheel that seems to float around the room," says Robin.

"Me too. It's so beautiful," I say.

"You used to dance with Amala, didn't you?" asks Bea.

"Yeah," I say through a mouthful of salad.

"What was it like?"

"It was fun," I say, "but nothing like Dana's studio."

Robin laughs. "Well, of course. That's why all the best students end up with Dana."

I glance at Angela crouching in the dirt, her long elegant fingers stroking a leafy green plant. "Yeah, I guess," I say.

Robin must have followed my gaze and my thoughts because she says, "I hear Angela's really good too."

"She's a natural," I say.

"So how come she's not dancing with Dana?"

I shrug. "She wasn't invited."

"Dana's very picky, but she always chooses well. She must have seen something in you that she didn't see in Angela. I bet she could come dance with Dana if she really wanted to. If she worked hard enough," Robin says.

I don't know what Angela really wants. I thought she wanted to dance more than anything, like I do, but in the last few days I've begun to wonder. She doesn't seem to want to hear about Dana's classes, and now she says she's going to skip dance class to hang out with Jonas.

She'll never be a professional dancer. Not if she skips classes and stuff. That's not the way to further her dance career. It really isn't.

Eight

"Again!" Dana says, and the twelve of us take up our starting positions. I could do this part blindfolded, I think as I count out the beats and move into action. It's my second week, and only my third class, but I've been practicing so much I feel like I've been working on this dance forever.

"One and two and three and..." calls Dana from the front of the room.

We're working on a short sequence toward the end of the song, and the timing is tricky. I end up moving forward too soon. Dana stops the music and says, "Lila, your timing is off!" We try again. Two minutes later she calls out, "Lila, your timing!" I grit my teeth and focus on counting the steps in my head.

For the next section of the music, the twelve of us split into four groups. Bea, Eve and Sam do a wide hip circle, twirl to face the back of the room and fast shimmy for three beats, then twirl back to the front and...oops, Bea trips in the twirl and stumbles ever so slightly.

Dana stops the music. "Again!" she calls.

Eve's face is creased with frustration as they go through the short sequence again. "Two *and* three and," she counts as they start the shimmy. Bea gets it right this time, and they move from the twirl into a figure eight in the hips. Their right hips sway from back to front, and then they shift their weight to their right legs as their left hips sway from back to front.

But once again Bea messes up. Eve throws up her arms, and Dana says, "Get some water, everyone, while I work with Bea on this."

Bea's face is scarlet as we all move to the edges of the room.

Eve has that brittleness about her again, and when we meet next to the water bottles, she sighs heavily. For the whole time we wait for Dana and Bea to run through the sequence, Eve never takes her eyes off Bea. Man, the girl is focused. I guess

47

that's what makes her such a good dancer. But I hope she never turns that look on me. It makes me shiver to think about it.

We stop several more times through the class. Three more times for Bea and a couple more times for me. It's like I can't do anything right today. By the end of class our nerves are ragged, and we're all sweating like pigs.

"Good work today, girls," Dana says as we file out of the room.

"Phew, she's tough," I say to Robin as we pull on our shoes.

"Yeah, don't you like it?" she asks.

I sigh and then take a deep breath. "I love it," I say. "Maybe not at the moment, as she's drilling me in a movement over and over and over again, but later, when I get it, then I love it."

"Me too," says Robin. "She's made me the dancer I am."

"I know what you mean. Dana doesn't put up with any sloppiness. Like how she's always getting us for posture and stuff."

"Exactly," says Robin.

She waves goodbye as she leaves the room, and I pull on my sweater and gather my bag.

As I walk past the door to the studio, I see Eve and Bea in the room, talking to Dana. I wonder what they're talking about. I don't think I'd want to be part of that conversation.

* * *

At Monday's class, it's clear that Bea has spent her whole weekend practicing, and even Eve seems pleased with her after our first run-through. I practiced a lot too, so Dana only has to stop for me once to go over the muscles I should be using in my chest lifts. I concentrate really hard on using my upper back and upper abs in the proper sequence as we go through the choreography a second time. Dana doesn't say anything, but by this time I've learned that's a good thing.

When we break, I find myself standing next to Bea, so between gulps of water I say, "You danced beautifully today, Bea."

She beams at me and says, "Robin and Alex and I got together on the weekend to practice. They drilled me, and I'm feeling pretty good."

"That was nice of them," I say.

"Yeah, they were so helpful. I don't want to get kicked out now."

"Dana wouldn't do that," I say, but Bea cocks her eyebrow at me and says, "She might. And Eve wouldn't mind if she did."

"I'm sure that's not true," I say, but Bea grimaces, and I think of the conversation I saw at the end of last class between Bea, Eve and Dana. Probably that's what it was about.

"Well, anyway, you looked great just now," I say. "I'm sure she won't kick you out."

"Thanks, Lila."

We put our water bottles down and head back to the center of the room. As I stretch and settle into my posture for the next run-through, I glance over at Robin. I wish they had included me in their weekend sessions.

By the end of class, I feel like I could perform this dance for the queen. Every move, every gesture, feels familiar and right. I'm breathing fast and sweating hard, but it's a relief to know the dance so well.

As we gather up our water bottles and head toward the door to the lobby, Eve puts her hand on my shoulder and says, "You're really coming along,

Lila. I'm glad Amala sent you over. You have a good chance of being one of the girls chosen to perform in the festival."

"What?" I ask stupidly. "Aren't we all going to?"

Eve tosses her ponytail over her shoulder and arches her eyebrows at me. "Ten of us are," she says.

There are twelve of us.

My face must give away my confusion, because Eve says, "Didn't you know you were being auditioned?"

I shake my head, because I can't speak. I feel like such an idiot. There I was, so happy that Dana was giving me all that attention, correcting tiny aspects of posture or gesture, and proud of myself for learning the dance so quickly, when all along she's been sussing me, trying to decide if I'm going to be one of the girls who gets cut from the troupe for the performance.

"It makes sense," Eve goes on as we enter the lobby and she pulls her hoodie and shoes out of the cupboard. "I mean, of course Dana wants more girls than she needs, so she can choose the best ones. It's how any professional

51

dance group works." She zips up her hoodie and slips on her shoes.

The lightness I felt at the end of class disappears, and my boots feel like they're made of concrete as I shuffle down the stairs behind Eve and out of the building to the bus stop. For the whole ride home, all I can think about is what a dolt I've been. It makes me sick to my stomach to think about it.

Nine

I toss and turn all night, dreaming I'm in dance class and that at every beat of the music Dana stops me to correct my posture or movement. Each time, I'm sure I'm standing or moving properly, but when I look down, I'm all wrong, and I have two left feet, and I'm dressed like a construction worker with overalls and tools hanging from my pockets. It makes the night seem to last forever, and in the morning I have to drag myself out of bed, and I miss the first bus again. When I slide into the seat next to Angela in English, she says, "Ouch. What happened to you?"

"I have so much to tell you," I say.

"Me too," she says.

It's hard to pay attention in class because I'm so tired, and twice Angela nudges me awake. I try to talk to her at lunch, but Nini and Sarit don't get the hint that we want to be alone, and they chat at us for the whole hour. Angela keeps looking at me funny across the picnic table, which must be because I keep nodding off, and by the time school is out, all I want to do is head home for a nap. Thank goodness there's no dance class tonight.

Angela has to talk to Mrs. O'Connor about her *To Kill a Mockingbird* essay, so I head to the study lounge to wait for her. I haven't even started my essay. I guess now's a good time, but my eyes are so blurry that even though I stare at the page until Angela comes to find me, I have no idea what the instructions say.

"So," I say once we're settled on the bus. "It turns out Dana is only going to have ten girls on the stage, not twelve, so all this time, she's been auditioning me. I can hardly believe it! There I was, being so proud that she was paying all that attention to me when all along she was checking me out. Every time she corrected my footwork I'd think, She's paying attention to me to make me perfect, but actually she was noticing how sloppy my footwork was."

"I'm sure that's not true, Lila. I'm sure she was trying to make you perfect."

"You think? You don't think she was looking for how terrible a dancer I am?"

"Of course not! I heard Dana say she approved of you as Amala's choice to go dance with her. I know she thinks you're a great dancer. She wouldn't have you there if she didn't, would she? I mean, she's trying to put together the best-possible troupe for the festival, so even if she is only taking ten of the twelve girls, those twelve girls have to be the best around."

"Yeah, I guess you're right," I say. Angela's long hair falls into my shoulder, and I wrap my fingers in its silky smoothness. "It's so amazing, Angela, dancing with someone who's so thorough. I mean, sometimes it makes me panicky, like last night, but mostly, I admire her and the girls who dance with her so much. I don't know if I'm good enough, you know?"

"Of course you are," Angela says.

"I really hope I'm chosen. I mean, I should be, right? There are other girls in the class who aren't as good, who don't know the dance as well as I do even though they've been there longer. So I should be able to dance in the festival, don't you think?" I say.

"Of course," Angela says, but she pulls her hair away from me and slides over so we aren't touching.

"What?" I say.

She doesn't answer.

"Is something wrong?" I ask.

She still doesn't answer.

"There is something wrong. What is it?" I ask.

Angela slides even farther down the seat and says, "You've spent the whole bus ride complaining about your issues, and you haven't even asked me how my date with Jonas went."

"I'm so sorry, Angela! I totally forgot! How'd it go?"

"You can't just ask me now and make it okay. There are things I need to talk to you about, and you've been so caught up with your dancing you haven't even noticed," she says, and without warning, she stands up as the bus pulls into a stop and rushes out the door.

"Angela," I call, but she's gone. She marches down the street without once glancing up at the bus. For the rest of the ride home, my heart races, and I have to wipe tears from my eyes.

By the time we reach my stop and I get off the bus, all I can think about is figuring out what's going on with Angela. Her house is on the way to mine, so when I get there, I plunk myself down on her step to wait for her.

"I'm sorry," I say again when she comes up the driveway.

She hesitates, like she might turn around again, but instead she sits next to me on the step and puts her head in her hands.

"How was the date?" I ask.

"Wonderful," she says without raising her head.

"So...I don't get it. Why are you sitting with your head in your hands?"

"He wants to go out with me again," Angela says.

"But that's good, isn't it?"

Angela sits up and stretches. "Yeah, for sure. But the problem is Nini. She keeps going on about how much she's in love with him, and the truth is, he doesn't really like her—not like that. I don't want to hurt her feelings, and I don't want to lie to her, so I keep avoiding her, and now she thinks I'm mad at her because I won't talk to her. I don't know what to do." She drops her head into her hands again. "Nini's practically my best friend except for you. I can't keep lying to her," she says.

"What do you mean *lying*?" I ask.

"She asked me why I missed dance the other day, and I made up some excuse about helping my mom, which I totally think she didn't believe, because my mom knows I have dance on Wednesdays. And now I'm going to have to lie to her again."

"Why?"

"We're going skating this Wednesday. Nini's going to ask again."

"Wait! You're going to miss another dance class? Can't you go another night?"

"It's the only night he's free. His team is playing in some tournament all the other nights this week."

"So it's okay for you to skip class but it's not okay for him to miss a game?" I ask. My voice rises as I speak. I can't believe Angela is cutting out on dance class again.

"It's a practice. I'd never miss a performance, just like he'd never skip a game," Angela says.

"I can't believe you're missing another class," I say.

"That's not the point. The point is Nini."

"It is the point."

Angela sighs. "No it's not. Nini's more important. I don't want to lie to her, and I don't want to give up Jonas. What should I do?"

"I have no idea," I say. "I really don't. I don't know why you would even go out with a guy who makes you miss dance class, especially when the festival is only a few weeks away."

"You don't understand," she says.

"I gotta go home," I say.

Angela eyes me as I gather my bag and sweater. "Fat lot of help you are," she says as I stand up and step onto the path.

I shrug. "Get him to go another night. Easy peasy," I say.

"What about Nini?"

"You'll have to tell her sometime. Better make it now, before it goes too far."

Angela stands up and picks up her bag. "You don't get it," she says.

"You're right," I say. "I don't." And I walk down the path to the sidewalk.

Ten

Eve stands in the middle of the room, a fierce look on her face as she drills hip circles half time, then quarter time, then full time. I can see her through the doorway as I pull off my coat and boots and slip on my leg warmers. I skipped last period to come here early, hoping I'd be alone so I could practice in front of the mirror. After yesterday's fight with Angela, it was a good excuse to avoid her after school, and I also want to dance perfectly today.

Though I'm making a bit of noise, I don't think Eve notices, because her concentration never falters. Over and over she drills the same move, until her hip muscles must be tired, but the movement is flawless. As the song ends and another begins, her body shifts to meet the new tempo, and she somehow manages to stay on the right beat without making any jarring changes.

"Join me," she says when I come into the studio.

I walk across the dance floor to stand next to her. "I didn't think you heard me," I say.

She nods at me through the mirror and says, "Chest circles next, starting right."

I take a moment to settle into my posture, and then, on the beat, I slide my chest to the right, lift in the center, slide to the left and drop back to neutral. It's jerky at first, as I warm up, but after a couple of circles the movement smooths out. I can feel my upper abdominals and the muscles in my upper back working. It takes concentration to make sure each movement is made with the proper combination of muscles so that my lungs and diaphragm are clear and I can still breathe easily.

Eve and I practice together to the beat, our breathing following our bodies, so we look and sound like one being, separated by a foot of space. For a second I see the whole troupe standing here, all in colorful skirts and sparkly scarves. A whole row of girls moving as one. It will be spectacular.

I just hope I'm one of them.

The image only lasts a second, and then I'm back to seeing Eve and me standing in our tank tops and yoga pants and leg warmers, with sweat on our faces. The song ends, and Eve turns and hugs me.

"Oh," I say, because I didn't expect that. Eve always seems so distant.

She laughs and says, "Let's go again, this time with hips."

"Aren't the others going to get here soon?" I ask.

"We'll stop when they do."

I really hadn't expected to find her here, but it makes sense, so I ask, "Do you come before every class to practice?"

Eve nods. "It's my secret strategy for success." She's still smiling like we've won a competition.

"How come you're so happy?" I ask.

Eve turns away from me slightly, so she's not looking at me as she says, "I've waited a long time to find someone as serious about dance as I am. I'm glad it's you. You could be really, really good, you know."

I don't know how to respond to that. On the one hand, she's saying I'm not that good, but on the other, I know she means to compliment me.

"Thanks, I think."

"Okay, let's go again!" Eve jumps around me in a totally un-Eve-like way, making me laugh along with her. After a second she stops, and we both settle back into posture until she nods at me and presses the remote, and we start a slow arm undulation.

By the time the rest of the girls come in, I'm tired but loosened up, and after a couple of sips of water I'm ready for class. Dana strides in and takes her position in front of the mirrors. We go through the warm-up quickly, then get into place and strike our starting poses. Dana starts the music.

The first girls move. I count the beats so that when my turn comes, I am in perfect time. My body glides through the motions until our sequence is over and the wave of movement flows along to the next batch of girls. When we all dance into the pinwheel, I am still in perfect time, and my footwork is flawless, so I don't lose any momentum when I step out for the shimmy. Eve grins at me as I position myself beside her and Bea, and I grin back.

The rest of the song goes smoothly. When we end, we all wait silently to digest what has happened. Dana always stands at the front of the room, watching with her hands on her hips, but today her hands are clasped in front of her chest like she's concentrating really hard.

"Girls, that was amazing!" she says.

Something inside me softens when she says that, and I realize I've been clenching my jaw for days. I let out a little whoop. The girls laugh, but then join me, and the twelve of us whistle and jump around until Dana says, "Let's see if you can do it again."

That sobers us up, but there are still grins on our faces as we settle into our poses and wait for the music. This time Dana is back to stopping us as we run through, but she only stops for me once, thankfully, and I breathe easier as we come to the last beat.

When the music ends, Dana says, "I have news."

All the tension returns, because this is going to be the moment. I glance around. Who is she going to cut? Robin's face is beet red, and Bea pulls at a lock of her hair. Alex stares at her toes. Only Eve stares boldly at Dana. But then Dana says, "I've chosen the costume for the dance, and I have a sample here to show you."

I let out a breath I didn't know I was holding and feel my jaw relax again. Robin's face goes back to its normal color, and Bea lets go of her hair. Dana walks to the doorway and reaches up to a suit bag hanging off it. She unzips it slowly, as if to prolong the suspense, then reaches in and pulls out the costume.

The skirt is white, straight from the hips to a slight flare at the bottom, and threaded in gold so it sparkles. Dana pulls it on over her leggings and straightens it, then kicks out a leg, showing off the long slit that starts mid-thigh. Next, she pulls a belt out of the bag. It's white, as wide as my hand and banded in gold studs. Dana wraps it around the top of the skirt, adjusting both so they sit low on her hips. When she pulls off her tights, we get the full effect of the skirt: shimmery but slinky.

"That'll look amazing on you," I say to Eve, who's standing next to me.

"On all of us," she says.

I nod, but yeah, it'll look better on her than on anyone else.

Dana reaches into the bag again and pulls out a piece of cloth that she unravels to reveal a white bra studded with gold threads and beads.

Robin and Alex gasp beside me as Dana pulls off her tank top and straps herself into the bra. She shakes her hair out of its elastic and raises her arms to show us the full effect of the bra.

"We'll wear gold jewelry to give some color," she says.

Eve's eyes sparkle, and I can see why. She's got the perfect body for this costume. Slim, tall and busty. The rest of the girls look less excited, and both Alex and Bea have concern in their eyes.

"It's pretty skimpy," I whisper to Robin. She nods without taking her eyes off Dana.

"What do you think, girls?" Dana asks.

"Fantastic," says Eve.

"I knew you'd like it," Dana says with a big grin at Eve. "What about the rest of you? Alex, Sam?"

Alex and Sam both nod and smile, but Bea says, "It's different than usual."

"Indeed. I thought we'd try for a new style. I want us to really stand out this time, and this costume is so flashy," says Dana.

"I don't know if I'll be able to keep a bra like that up," says Allie from behind me, and we all laugh. Allie's flat as a board.

But Dana says, "We'll have a bra-making party. Buy yourself a white bra, and we'll build up from there. We take off all the straps and make our own ties, so they are super adjustable, and we cover the bras in satin and beads and coins so they look flashy. This style can fit everyone. You're all going to be so beautiful and stylish. We'll wear hair down and flowing. You'll see—it'll look amazing."

The costume is beautiful, but my heart races, because it hits me that I will be up onstage in a skimpy bra and a nearly-as-skimpy skirt, and despite what she says, I'm not sure that I am going to be beautiful and stylish. I may look like a lumpy ghost. For a second, I long for both Angela's dark coloring and Amala's bright costume. Just for a second.

Eleven

That night I dream of dancing again. This time I'm wearing the right costume, but when I walk onto the stage, the bra snaps open and falls off, and I'm left topless in front of everyone I know. I wake with a start. My sheets are all tangled at the bottom of the bed, and I'm drenched in sweat. My heart is racing. It only takes me a second to scroll down to Angela's name, but then I stare at my phone for a while before turning it off and lying back down. I want to talk to Angela more than anything. I'm not sure if she'll want to talk to me.

In the morning I get up in time to catch the bus, and I sprint to the stop and hop on a second before it pulls away. I make my way down the aisle and wait for Angela to get on at the next stop.

"What are you studying?" I ask as she pulls out her books. Her stuff spills across the seat, so I have to squish myself in next to her to sit down.

"English," she says.

"Oh no! I totally forgot about the English test. Something more to worry about."

Angela sighs. "What are you worried about?"

Now that she's asked, I'm not sure I want to talk about it, so I say, "Dance."

"I figured, but what specifically?"

She still sounds grumpy, almost like she was expecting me to complain, so I don't say anything until she says, "Lila? If you don't have anything to say, I'm going to get back to studying."

"It's the costume," I say. "I hate it."

"I thought you always loved Dana's costumes," Angela says.

"Usually, yeah, but this one's different. It's all white and gold. It'll make me look like a ghost. Plus, the skirt has a huge slit up the side, and"—I take a deep breath, because this is really the part I have a problem with—"the top's a bra."

I expect Angela to gasp or something, but she blinks and says, "A bra?"

I nod.

"Ouch," she says.

"Yeah."

"I like Amala's costume better," I say.

"Yeah. I love it," Angela says. "It's not really professional-looking though."

"What's that supposed to mean?"

"Nothing. Forget it," she says. She points her nose back into her book, and I am left staring at the top of her head.

Angela isn't sympathetic in the least. How'd she feel if she had to wear a stupid white skirt and a bra?

* * *

The English test is hard, and I know I haven't done well. When it's over I head to the garden to wait for Angela to join me, but today when she comes, she's with Jonas and Nini. So I guess she hasn't said anything to Nini yet.

"You finished quickly," Jonas says to me.

"Yeah." I don't want to talk about the test, because I know I failed, so I don't pay much attention as Nini and Angela and Jonas go over the answers they gave. Besides, Jonas spends the whole time trying to make Angela look at him, Angela spends the whole time looking at everyone except him, and Nini spends her whole time looking at him and trying to get him to look at her. Lovely. I so don't want to be part of that.

After a few minutes of trying to ignore the conversation, I give up and leave. I'm halfway across the courtyard when I spot Robin and Alex. "Hey, Robin," I call, jogging to catch up with them. "Where are you two going?"

"Alex wants samosas," Robin says.

There's a bakery down the street that sells French bread, Danish pastries and Indian samosas.

"Can I come?" I ask.

"Sure," Robin says, and we head out of the courtyard and onto the street. "Did you hear about Bea?" she asks.

"What about her?"

"She told Dana she quit."

"What? No way! How come?" I ask.

"Are you really surprised?" Alex says. "Dana picks on her all the time. Bea told Dana she feels like she's not good enough to dance for her."

"What did Dana say?"

"She said Bea has promise, but she's not applying herself."

"That's so unfair!" I say. I know both Alex and Robin have practiced a lot with Bea in the last couple of weeks.

"I know," says Robin.

"So she quit?"

"I guess Dana tried to convince her to stay, but Bea said her mom wants her to go to another studio," Alex says.

We reach the bakery and walk inside. The air is warm and smells of fresh bread. I inhale deeply.

"Wow," I say. Bea's quitting is big news. I've always liked Bea, and though she has a hard time learning the moves, she's really a beautiful dancer. Her movements are fluid and graceful. It's not her fault Dana rides her so much that it makes her nervous and then she messes up. Quitting though. That's big.

The bakery is busy with kids from our school, and I lower my voice so only Robin and Alex can hear. "Which studio is she going to?"

"Probably Amala's," Robin says.

"Yeah, that's where Angela dances. Bea'll love it there!" I say.

For some reason, my voice catches as I say it, but neither Robin nor Alex notices, and Alex says, "I hope she does. I'm going to miss her."

Robin reaches the front of the line and orders three samosas. It takes us a minute to figure out the cash, and once we've paid, we stand over to the side to wait for the samosas to be heated up.

"The truth is that she wouldn't have been performing with us anyway," Robin says after a long moment. "She was bound to be one of the girls who got cut. This way she makes it her choice, not Dana's. So good for her."

"Maybe Dana wouldn't have cut her," I say.

Both Robin and Alex raise their eyebrows at me, and I shrug in agreement. Bea was going to be one of the girls cut.

"Who else is going to get cut?" Alex asks.

"Not you," Robin says. "Or you, Lila."

The bakery lady hands us our samosas, and I quickly bite into mine and head for the door so I don't have to respond. When Robin and Alex catch up with me outside, I say, "What do you think about Bea's brother, Jonas? He's in my English class."

"H. O. T.," says Alex, and just like that, we're talking about boys. We slow down as we go over all the boys in our grade, and by the time we get back to school, I'm feeling more relaxed than I have all day.

Twelve

But no matter what Robin and Alex or anyone else says, I can't help but wonder if I'm going to be one of the girls who gets cut. It's all I think about during math and socials, and even on the bus ride home when Nini and Sarit try to get me to talk about Mrs. O'Connor, I agree with them without really listening to what they're saying.

There's no dance class this afternoon, so I get on my bike and ride around thinking. Right now things aren't great. I know I've failed my English test, and I haven't handed in my essay yet, and I haven't had a good night's sleep in at least a week, and I'm probably going to get cut from Dana's troupe. I bike around for a while until I find myself at Angela's door. I didn't plan it;

I just ended up here. Of all the things worrying me right now, the one I hate the most is being in a fight with Angela. It's even worse than not knowing what's going to happen with dance.

Angela's mom opens the door before I have a chance to knock. Her hair's coming loose from its bun, and there's a big chocolate smear across her left cheek.

"We're making brownies," she says, and we both break into laughter because for years and years we've had a joke that I can smell her brownies from my house and come running. My legs knew bringing me here was the best thing for me, even if my brain didn't.

"Hi, Lila," Angela says when I follow her mother into the kitchen. I sit in my usual chair and Angela's mom hands me a spoon to lick. The chocolaty goodness fills my mouth, and when I'm done I stand next to Angela's mom and try to stick my finger into the mixture. She smacks my hand away playfully.

"So what's up these days, Lila?" Angela's mom asks.

"Lila's dancing with Dana, Mom, remember?" Angela says.

I nod, and Angela's mom says, "I know, but how's it going? Are you enjoying it? Don't you miss Amala and the girls?"

"Dana's very professional, and Lila's learning a lot," Angela says. She flashes me a huge smile when she says this. There's no trace of jealousy or sarcasm in her voice, and I realize all at once that Angela is truly pleased for me. Even though I've been selfish, she really does want me to succeed.

Tears form in my eyes.

"Lila?" Angela's mom says. She puts down her spoon and runs her hands over my hair as she pulls me into a hug. "What's wrong, sweetie?"

"I'm not sure about it. I mean, about the class, about Dana, about any of it."

"I thought you loved how professional Dana is," Angela says.

"I did. I do. I don't know. I did, but then Bea quit because Dana rides her so hard. She's a good dancer—Bea, I mean—but Dana pushed her so hard that she was nervous all the time, so she made mistakes. And I always loved how Dana would correct every tiny bit of movement, because I thought she was helping us, but now I don't know." The words tumble out of my mouth.

"Isn't she helping?" Angela's mom asks.

I shake my head. "I don't know what she wants. I mean, we work so hard. I know for a fact that Bea practiced way more than anyone else, and Dana tells her she isn't applying herself. What does she want? We can't quit school and dance full time."

"Does she do that to you too?" Angela's mom asks.

I let out a deep breath. "Yeah, sometimes."

"So you feel like you're being criticized, not helped?"

"I'm starting to." There. I've said it.

Angela's mom turns back to the bowl and stirs again. After a couple of fast swirls she pours the mixture into the pans waiting on the counter. When the trays are full she hands the bowl to me. Then she reaches across the counter and pulls three spatulas from the pile. She gives one to me and one to Angela.

"Chocolate therapy," she says.

The three of us dig into the bowl, scraping leftover chocolate-brownie batter onto the spatulas, then licking them. Soon our faces are even more covered in chocolate, and when there's not enough left in the bowl for spatulas, I use my finger until my hand is sticky and my stomach tells me it's time to stop.

Angela puts the two brownie pans into the oven and turns on the timer.

"I'll wash up, girls," her mom says. "You two go do something fun. I'll let you know when the brownies are ready."

"Thanks, Mom," Angela says, giving her mom a kiss on the cheek.

"You're being really nice to me," I say to Angela when we get to her room.

"You sound surprised," she says.

I can't look at her as I say, "I was kinda selfish, and I thought you were mad at me."

"I am, but also I'm your best friend. BFFs, remember? We need to help each other when we're in trouble," Angela says.

"Are you in trouble? Are you being nice to me so I'll be nice to you?"

"No, idiot!" Angela frowns and plunks herself on her bed. "You're the one in trouble, remember. You didn't study for English at all, did you? And every day you seem more and more tired. So something must be going on."

"I just told you," I say, sitting next to her.

"Dana's costume and whether or not you'll get picked? That's it, really? That's making you so stressed you can't sleep?"

It's like Angela and I are talking two different languages. "Of course it's making me stressed. Wouldn't it stress you out?"

"A bit, I guess," she says.

"All I've ever wanted was to dance. That's all. Is that too much to ask?" I say.

Angela looks at me like maybe I came from Mars. Then, out of the blue, she says, "Do you remember Amala's choreography?"

"I think so."

"Run through it with me. I need the practice," Angela says.

"That's because you've been skipping classes to hang out with Jonas," I say with what I hope is a light tone.

"Amala's okay with it, you know. I talked to her, and she said as long as I keep practicing at home and I come to the last rehearsals before the festival, she's okay with me missing a couple of classes," Angela says.

"Really? I can't imagine Dana saying something like that."

"So come on; practice with me. I promised Amala I'd do it every day."

It's not what I want to do, but then again, maybe dancing will make me feel better. "Okay," I say.

Angela jumps across the room and puts her phone on the stand. She fiddles for a second, then says, "Ready?"

I scramble into position. "Ready."

The music starts. It begins with the drums calling the other instruments, which join one by one as Angela and I snake our arms around us, building energy. Then the drums trill and we twirl, almost bumping into each other in the small space. The sequence of hip drops and kicks comes back to me as we do them, and when the bit with the fast hip and chest lifts starts, Angela and I both nail the transition. The music pauses, then builds from slow to fast. Angela and I pick up our shimmies starting at the hips and moving up to our shoulders. The music takes over my whole body, and I stop thinking and start feeling the beat within me, moving every inch of my body.

The music slows, and we catch the wave of sound with a body roll, drawing the music down from the air and through our bodies to the floor. We do a slow twirl, come back to the front and end.

"Wow! I can't believe you remembered all that," Angela says when the music stops.

"I can," I say. "I love that choreography, and the music." I flop onto the bed, which is a bad idea, because from here I can see Angela's beautiful costume hanging on the back of her cupboard.

"I do too. And I wish you were dancing it with us."

"I..." There's a crash about to happen in my mind, which I know I can't do anything about. I can feel it coming, so I study the tiny mirrors on Angela's costume, counting them one by one, but the crash comes anyway, and suddenly I'm faced with the thought that I was happier when I danced with Amala. I think I've known this deep down for a while, but now I can't hide from it anymore. Not with her music and choreography still in my body. It makes my throat tight to think about it.

"You...?" says Angela.

"Nothing. I love that music. I'd forgotten, that's all."

Thirteen

The room is quieter than usual when Dana walks in on Saturday morning. We're practicing every day now, since the festival is only a week and a half away. We're all standing in our positions, which means we can't help seeing the huge hole where Bea used to be. I'm not the only one who keeps glancing at the empty spot.

Dana surveys us from the front of the room, then says, "Eve, Sam, both of you move closer to each other by about a foot."

The two girls each take a step toward each other.

"There we go," says Dana.

"We're off balance with two," Sam says.

She points to the other clusters of girls, but Dana says, "We're going to have four groupings, three of three and one of two."

No one responds with words, but suddenly there's a stiffness to the way most of us are standing. We glance at each other, and I know we're all wondering who's going to be next to go, and what the groupings will look like then.

We drill for the whole class, stopping frequently to make corrections in the new formation. On the surface it's the same as ever, but underneath something has shifted. It seems like we're not as friendly as usual tonight.

When the class is over, Dana says, "Good work, ladies. You are all beautiful dancers, and don't you forget it."

I catch the bus home with Robin and Alex. None of us says much until Robin asks, "If we're all such beautiful dancers, how come she has to choose only ten of us?"

It's what we've all been thinking, I know.

"I think it's a rule of the festival—only ten on the stage at a time," Alex says, but I say, "It can't be, because Amala has eleven dancing for her."

"Oh," says Alex. "Well, I just wish Bea hadn't quit."

"Yeah," I say.

Robin sighs. "Me too."

We're silent again as we pass another couple of bus stops.

Robin and Alex get off at their usual stops, but I get off near the high school and transfer to another bus. I need to talk to Amala.

* * *

The route is familiar, and it should feel natural to step off outside Amala's studio and take the three steps to her door, but my hand shakes as I reach out to turn the knob, and the stairs to the second floor loom long above me. My breath fills my throat as I climb, and I almost turn around before I reach the top, but as I come to the last step, Amala opens the door.

"Lila, what a lovely surprise!" she says. She's carrying the jug she uses to water the plants. There's a little wall alcove at the top of the stairs, next to the door to the lobby, and she always has flowers growing in it.

"These anthuriums are not thriving. Maybe I need to change them for something else," she says as she pours water into the bowl.

It's warm and sunny up here, and when I take my shoes off, the wood floors feel smooth under my feet. Amala smiles at me, and my breathing slows to a normal rate.

"I was hoping you'd come by to tell me about dancing with Dana," Amala says. "I hear her choreography is really something. And she showed me the costume. Stylish!"

I nod.

"Has Angela shown you her costume? I think the girls like it, and they look fantastic, especially Angela. The troupe's like a carnival, or a rhododendron garden."

"It's beautiful. I saw the costumes before I left, and yes, Angela showed me hers," I say. I don't say how much more I like Amala's costumes than Dana's. How I wish I looked like a part of the rhododendron garden rather than a pale ghost.

Amala finishes fiddling with the plants, and I follow her into the studio. A bar of sunlight stretches across the floor, splitting the room in two. Dust particles float in the air. There's a rack of skirts hanging along the far wall, with colorful piles of hip scarves underneath it. Amala has written step patterns in grease paint on the mirror. The warmth and friendliness of the room rushes at me and hits me with a whomp that takes my breath away.

Amala pulls a remote out of her waistband and turns on some music I don't recognize. She lowers the volume but raises her arms and does a three-step with a shimmy across the room.

"Warm up with me, Lila. We can talk and warm up at the same time," she says.

I follow her across the room, the movement coming slowly at first, until my muscles relax.

"So tell me all about it. How do you like the studio space? Have you made friends with the other girls? What do you like best about it? Isn't Dana the most beautiful dancer?" Amala tosses all these questions at me at once as we circle the room. She's ahead of me, but as we come around the circle, suddenly we're both facing the mirror, and she stops. Her hands drop and she turns to me.

"Lila, honey?" she says, and that's all it takes. I burst into tears.

"What is it?" Amala stops the music and sits down on the floor. She takes my hand and pulls me down next to her. "It's not working out for you?" she asks.

I shake my head. I don't want to speak while my voice is caught up in my tears, so I take a few deep breaths and then say, "I don't know if I should stay there, Amala."

She squeezes my hand and says, "Did you know Dana was my teacher for a while?"

"Really? You're so different in your dance style," I say.

"Yeah, but that doesn't mean I didn't learn from her."

"Did you..." I'm not sure how to ask this question, because I know Dana and Amala are friends. "Did you like being in her class?" I finally ask.

Amala doesn't answer. Instead, she stands up and does a complicated chest circle on top of a figure eight. Her arms and fingers weave elegantly around her. "Dana taught me that. She was the one who showed me how to use my fingertips when dancing," Amala says. "But," she adds, sitting down again, "I hated her classes."

She laughs, and because I'm so surprised, I laugh too, but then I say, "So you chose me to go to a place you hated?"

That hurts. Ouch, that hurts.

"That's not it at all. Lila, I've watched you dance since you were a little girl, and you, more than anyone else, love to dance. It's in everything you do, every move you make. You are a real dancer."

My face glows to hear those words. "What about Angela?" I ask.

"Angela too. Angela moves like a bird in flight; she's a natural. But what does Angela want out of dance?" Amala says.

"She just loves to dance," I say, because it's true. For Angela it's as simple as that. She wants to dance.

"And what do you want?" Amala asks.

That's not something I can answer quickly, so I lean back on my hands and stare at the ceiling for a second while responses swirl in my mind. Finally I say, "I thought I wanted to be a professional dancer."

"Exactly," says Amala.

"So you sent me to Dana because you thought she would help me with that?" I ask.

Amala nods and says, "Dana's hard. She's tough. But many of her girls have gone on to have good careers as dancers, and I wanted you to have a taste of that kind of life. I thought Dana's studio was the best place for you."

The door opens and a little girl walks into the room. She stops when she sees us, but Amala says, "Come on in, Pearl. Grab yourself a hip scarf. Are the other girls out there?"

Pearl nods and dashes across the room to take her pick of the scarves.

"Five-year-olds. Soooo cute," Amala whispers to me. "Want to help with the class?"

"I should go," I say.

The cuteness factor rises a whole lot as the rest of the girls rush into the room.

"Nice to see you, Lila," Amala says. She blows me a kiss and turns her attention to the little girls as I leave.

I've got a lot to think about.

Fourteen

On Sunday morning my mom asks me to help with the big spring cleaning she's planned for the afternoon. I sigh, but mostly because she expects me to. Really, I don't mind helping. I need time doing something with my hands so I can think.

Mom's already deep into cleaning when I get back from the morning's dance class. There's a pile of large rubber boxes by the front door, all labeled—things like *Winter clothes* or *Blankets—living room*—and the smell of chemically manufactured lemon scent hits my nose and makes me sneeze. Joni Mitchell's voice fills the air.

Mom staggers into the hallway carrying a way-too-huge potted plant.

"Whoa...what are you doing?" I ask.

"Taking this to the shower," she says through clenched teeth.

I drop my bag and grab the bottom of the pot.

"Oh, thanks!" she says. We lurch our way down the hallway to the bathroom, and with a heave we place the huge pot in the bathtub. Mom turns on the shower and lets the water run over the leaves of the plant. In seconds it goes from dusty and sickly to shiny and fresh.

"I like to let them think they're out in a forest every once in a while, like rain's really falling on their leaves," Mom says.

Coming from anyone else, that would sound totally crazy, but my mom knows plants don't think. She says things like that to make me smile.

"We'll let that dry before we take it back. Come help me get the next one," she says.

"Mom, can I at least take off my coat and have a bite to eat before I jump into housecleaning?"

Mom laughs. "Sure. There's mac and cheese in the oven for you."

I escape to the front hall, where I take off my coat and retrieve my bag before heading into the kitchen for a big bowl of mac and cheese smothered in ketchup. Yum.

There are two messages on my phone, one from Angela that says **@ Jonas's house. Me + him.** ☺ **Telling Nini this aft.** ☹

I text back, **Stay strong!**

The next message is from Robin: **Impromptu dance practice @ my place, 2 pm.**

One second later the doorbell rings, and I hear Mom open the door. "It's Robin, isn't it? Come in."

"Hi. Is Lila here?"

"Hi, Robin," I say as I come into the hallway. "I just got your text. I have to stay home and help my mom with some cleaning."

"We can wait a while to get started if you want," Robin says.

"I think this'll take a while. Mom's even cleaning the plants," I say with a laugh. Mom opens her mouth to speak, and I know she's going to say I can help her later, but I cut her off. "Also, I promised Angela I'd get together with her later this aft." Not true, but it sounds perfect. Both Robin and Mom believe me right away, and Robin says, "Okay. See you tomorrow then" and leaves.

"I'm glad you're hanging out with Angela this afternoon, Lila. We haven't seen much of her lately. Make sure to invite her for dinner. I'll make her favorite," says Mom.

She's got pollen smeared across her cheek. I reach over and rub it away. "I will," I say.

Made that bed. Now I have to lie in it.

* * *

When I've finished my mac and cheese and changed into some old jeans and a T-shirt, Mom shows me where to start cleaning. It's a bookshelf under the stairs to the basement, and it looks like no one's dusted it for twenty years. The first shelf is so dusty, I'm sneezing halfway through it.

"Don't forget to dust the books themselves," Mom says as she heads back upstairs.

"I won't," I say. I know the drill. We do this every year. I think I was even the person who dusted this shelf last time.

Thank goodness for headphones. Goodbye, Joni Mitchell. The thing about headphones is that you can listen to music without anyone else knowing. If Mom knew I was listening to the song Amala's class is dancing to, she would have questions.

Ever since I saw Amala yesterday I've been thinking about her studio and how much I love it there. Walking into that room made me remember how much I used to love dancing. *Used to.* I didn't even realize I wasn't loving it anymore until I was in there with her, and then I remembered how much fun we had. When did dance stop being fun? Is it supposed to be fun? Can it be fun and still get me where I want to go?

That's the basic question. Can dance be fun and still get me where I want to go?

The music soars into my headphones, and without me even thinking, my body dances. I shimmy and twirl and undulate as I dust, until the song is over.

Why do I have to make this choice? Everyone thinks I should stay with Dana. Even Amala. Even Mom. But does Dana? And do I want to?

Part of me wants to go back to Amala's studio. I want to dance with Angela and Nini and Sarit, to giggle in the breaks with them, to laugh when we screw up, to enjoy the colors and sounds around us. I don't want to be like Eve, taking dance so seriously that I neglect everything else, including my schoolwork. I don't want to be stressed out about dance.

But—and this is the big thing—I also want to be a professional dancer.

I put on the song we're dancing to at Dana's studio to remind myself that I love that music too. And the choreography. It's true. I do. I love the movements and how we all know them so well after all that practice. Dana has taught me many things, like how to count with better precision and how to hold my posture even in the middle of difficult moves and how to layer feet, hips, chest and arms all at once. But have I learned enough?

This whole thing might not be my choice anyway. Dana might tell me I'm not dancing in the festival with her, and then all of this will have been for nothing.

There's a thumping sound upstairs, and I'm relieved to hear Mom calling out for me to help her. My brain hurts. It's time to think about something else.

Fifteen

an u come over? I text to Angela. All that dusting has made my arms sore and my eyes itchy. Even Mom can see I need to take a break and get out of the basement.

YES! NEWS! she texts back.

It doesn't take her long to walk over, and when I open the door she barges in, heads straight upstairs to my bedroom, flops onto my bed and sighs. "Guess what?"

"Tell me," I say. I'm not in the mood for games.

"It's the best thing ever," she says.

"Oh." I sit down next to her and say, "You're coming to dance with Dana!"

"No! It's way better than that," Angela says.

Okay, better than that? What could it be? "Something to do with Jonas? He asked you out again?"

"Even better. His family invited me to go with them to Mexico."

"Wow! *Mexico!*" I leap across the bed and engulf Angela in a bear hug. She laughs and hugs me back. We struggle to standing, then laugh and jump and hug all around the room. "You've always wanted to go to Mexico," I say.

"And, even better, with Jonas. And I love his mom and dad. They're awesome," Angela says.

"And Bea. She's nice too."

Angela plops back down on the bed. "Bea's not coming. That's how come there's room for me."

"No way. How come she's not going?"

Angela stands up and walks over to my closet. She opens the door and examines herself in the mirror on the back of the door. "Promise you won't be mad when I say this?"

"How can I when I don't know what you're going to say?"

"Just promise."

"Okay, I won't be mad. I promise."

"Bea's not going because she decided to stay and perform with Amala's troupe at the festival. Amala says she's learned the choreography well enough to perform if she practices every day."

It takes a second for that to work through my brain, but when it does, the word "No!" escapes my mouth before I can stop it.

"You promised," Angela says.

"How can you?" I almost shout.

"Can't you understand, Lila? I told you, I *really* like Jonas, and he likes me too."

"But the festival..."

Angela comes back to the bed and sits beside me. "It's not the end of the world. There'll be other festivals."

"But...this is our dream. It's our first step to being professional dancers. You're making a mistake, Angela. There'll be other boys, but maybe we'll never be invited to another festival, and you'll have missed your opportunity to be seen by someone," I say.

Angela takes my hand and holds it to her heart. "Lila, being a professional dancer is your dream, not mine."

I pull my hand back. "Amala was telling me yesterday how much you love to dance."

"Yeah, I love to dance. But I love other things too. I guess you can't understand that," Angela says. "You know when you want something so much you can't even see anything else? That's how you are about dance. That's how you've been ever since you went to Dana's studio. I thought I knew you, Lila. I thought you'd be happy for me to have Jonas in my life. But instead you're mad that I'm missing a stupid dance performance. So what if someone never sees me? I'm happy dancing with Amala. That's all I ever wanted. You used to love it too until Dana got her claws into you."

"Her claws into me? If you mean corrected the sloppiness I got from dancing with Amala, then yeah, for sure."

"How can you say that? You loved dancing with Amala right up to the moment you got chosen to go to Dana's. You loved it and everything about it. And you loved Amala."

"I do love Amala. But that doesn't mean Dana's not better," I say.

"Dana's better so you get to say bad things about Amala? Like somehow you're better than the rest of us?"

I shrug.

"So that's what you think?" she asks.

"I think you're making a big mistake. How can you put a boy ahead of dance? And I bet you haven't even told Nini yet, have you?"

"Nini has nothing to do with it. Jonas doesn't even like her," Angela says.

"So you're better than her, is that it?"

Angela whips her head back like I slapped her in the face. "That was mean," she says. She picks up her bag, and without saying anything else, she walks through the door and down the stairs.

I don't follow her. The awful truth is that she is totally right. About everything.

I don't think I've ever felt this small.

Sixteen

"Right foot first," Dana says.

I managed to avoid Angela at school all day after our fight yesterday, but now I'm having a really hard time concentrating on what Dana is saying, and I keep messing up.

"The step's not that tricky," she says to me. "Your brain's making you think it is, but it's not. Imagine you have a box around you, and everywhere you move, that box stays the same. So if I say go right, no matter where in the room you are facing, you will always move to the right side of your box." Dana shows what she means by stepping out to her right, spinning to face the side of the room, stepping out to her right again, and this time spinning so she's facing the back of the room. "Make sense?" she asks.

I nod, and she says, "Again!" and this time when she starts the music, we all smoothly spin to the right of the room, to the back, to the left and back to the front.

"Excellent. Now let's do that in the song. We'll start from the beginning, and when we hit this point, remember that all you are doing is moving your box around you," Dana says.

The song starts out well. We all know this choreography like it's mapped in our toes, but when we get to the spins, somehow the stuff Dana said about a box doesn't make sense anymore, and even though I try turning to my right and spinning from there, I still end up facing the wrong direction at the end.

"No, no, no." Dana runs her hands through her hair. "No." She stands still and stares at the mirror for a long minute, then says, "We're making a change. We're going to cut that, and we'll do a repeat of the phrase before. I can't let you girls go out onstage like that. Twirls all over the place. No way."

It's hard not to catch anyone's eye when you're all standing in front of a mirror, but somehow I manage it. My face burns. My chest feels tight. This is my fault.

"Start from the beginning," Dana says. She marches to the side of the room and folds her arms like an army major. Everything starts well, but this time she stops us when we get to a spot where our arms snake around us. It's me again. I'm off count.

She points to my fingertips. "One and"—she points to my knuckle—"two and"—my wrist and elbow—"three and"—my shoulder—"four. Good. Try again. Good. And again." I go through it three times before she turns back to the front of the class and starts us up again.

Robin glares at me, and I know she's thinking, *Don't screw up now.* Dana's going to make her choice soon. Maybe even today.

When Dana turns off the music at the end of the class, I'm panting hard, and my body is stiff with tension. We all find our water bottles, and Dana says, "Well done, girls. I worked you hard today." She pauses, and we all turn to face her. We know what's coming. "The eleven of you are going to be the most exciting girls on the stage at the festival next week. Really, you all look fantastic," she says.

"Eleven?" asks Sam.

Dana nods.

"But I thought you were only choosing ten of us," Robin says.

"What? Of course not! Why would I do that? Good gracious, where did that idea come from?"

We all look at Eve, who turns a little pale and says, "Patricia from your Monday-night class said that."

"And you believed her? My goodness, how mean you must all think I am. I'm hurt that you would think that," Dana says. Her whole body droops in a very un-dancer-like way.

"No one's getting cut?" Eve asks.

Dana shakes her head. "No one. The performance is only a couple of days away. I'd never make a change like that this close."

"What about Bea then?" Robin asks.

Dana takes a big breath. "Bea is a good dancer, but she decided not to continue. It was her choice, though I blame myself for not encouraging her more."

"So we're all dancing together next week?" Alex asks.

"All together," Dana says.

The room erupts into laughter and yelps and hugs. Robin engulfs me in a huge bear hug, and Alex jumps on top of us so the three of us sway in a heap. I squeeze Robin and Alex back, and then the three of us clasp Sam and even Eve, though no one ever thought she'd be cut. She bear-hugs me back.

Alex and Sam start a polka across the room. Dana presses her remote so we have music, and soon we're all dancing freestyle, even Dana. She dances up to each of us in turn, and when she comes to me, she takes my hand and twirls me so we're back to back, and we do left-to-right undulations in opposition to each other. She winks as she heads over to Alex. All the tension that's been in the room ever since Bea left is gone, and we're all still laughing and busting out dance moves as we leave the studio.

We stand together waiting for our buses home. As the number seven pulls up and we climb on, Alex says, "That was the most fun class Dana's ever had."

"It was like one of Amala's classes," I say. "We're always breaking out in random acts of dancing."

We.

"You loved dancing with her, didn't you?" Alex says.

"Yeah, I did."

"More than Dana?" she asks.

But I don't know how to answer. I shrug and make my way to the back of the bus. When we reach my stop, I wave goodbye and walk down the street by myself. Everyone on the bus was so happy that we're all going to be dancing together. Everyone except me. Knowing that Dana wasn't being hard on me because she wanted to cut me from the troupe makes the whole thing a lot more difficult. Maybe I should stay with Dana. It's not as much fun, not by a long shot. She was hard on us today, really hard, but I've learned a lot from her. She's taught me how to use my muscles properly, how to hear the timing of the music with precision and how to focus my mind. She makes me sweat, but it's worth it...isn't it?

Now that Dana's not going to make that decision for me, I'm going to have to make it myself.

Seventeen

Last class before the festival, and we're all in our costumes. Eve looks spectacular, as we knew she would. I'm feeling uncomfortable with my sequin-and-lace-covered bra, but Mom helped me sew it and make sure it's secure. I'll get used to it.

"Again," says Dana, and she starts the music.

I can't get my head into it today, and already I've noticed Eve glaring at me, and when Dana stops the music and says, "Lila, posture," Eve rolls her eyes and breaks formation. She heads to the back of the room and picks up her water bottle.

"Sorry," I say to the class in general.

"The festival performance is in three days, Lila," Eve says when I reach past her for my water bottle.

"I know."

"So what are you doing?"

"Nerves, I guess. I'll get a good night's sleep. I'll be fine—don't worry." My voice comes out sounding more annoyed than I intended it to.

"Yeah, well, I am worried," Eve says. "We're meant to be acting like professionals, not falling apart."

"I thought we were supposed to be having fun," I say.

Eve shakes her head. "Well, that's where you're mistaken. This is my moment to shine, and I don't want you messing it up. You're a good dancer, Lila. Pull it together." She swigs her water and marches back to the center of the room.

I stand, stunned, where I am. *Wow.* I feel like she slapped me in the face.

"Let's go again, girls. We only have a couple more minutes before my next class starts. Let's try to get through in one run this time," Dana says.

I concentrate hard and make it through the dance without messing up. When the music ends, Dana says, "Well done, girls. I've worked you hard for the past few weeks, and I know it's been tough on some of you"—she glances at me—"but you look fantastic. Truly. You're going to stun the audience. So on Saturday, eat well in the morning, relax, and I'll see you at the theater an hour before curtain."

I still feel slapped as I put on my shoes, and when Robin asks me if I want to go to her house to run through the song a couple more times, I shake my head. I'm not sure what will happen if I open my mouth and try to speak, so I don't.

"You okay, Lila?" Robin asks.

Though my voice is shaky, I say, "Eve told me I need to *pull it together*. She doesn't want me messing things up for her tomorrow."

Robin leans across our bags and hugs me. "Ignore Eve. She's the one who's totally stressed out. She has no right to say that to you."

"Thanks, Robin," I say.

She keeps her arm around me as we walk out the door and onto the street. Alex joins us on the street, and the three of us get onto the bus. We're all pretty tired out from today's practice, so we're quiet as we ride along. When my stop comes, Robin says, "Sure you don't want to come over for more practice?"

"Yeah. I'm sure," I say.

There's only one thing I want to do, and that's talk to Angela.

* * *

Angela's mom answers the door. "Lila, what happened?" she asks. "Angela was so upset when she came back from your house the other day. She hasn't been herself ever since."

"I know," I say to my feet.

She wipes her hands on a tea towel and says, "I'll go see if she wants to talk to you."

From the hallway I can hear Angela's mom knocking and calling out, "Angela, Lila's here." I can't catch Angela's response, but her bedroom door opens, and Angela's mom walks inside the room, closing the door behind her. I lean into the hallway and try to breathe normally. I think I was about five the last time I had to wait here.

"Hi," Angela says a few minutes later when she comes down the stairs. She stands on the bottom step with her arms folded.

"I'm sorry," I say.

She doesn't move.

"I'm not better than you. Dana's not better than Amala," I say.

She shifts, so I add, "And the truth is, I'm confused about what I want. That's why I was being so mean. Because I was upset."

"I talked to Nini before I said I'd go to Mexico with Jonas's family," Angela says, still without unfolding her arms. "She was upset, but she said she understood."

"Okay." I still don't understand how she can go away instead of dancing in the festival, but I don't say that.

"And I talked to Amala too."

"What did she say?"

"She said you never can tell where your heart is going to take you, and that I should definitely follow my heart."

I take a step toward her and say, "But you love dancing. You've always loved dancing."

"But not performing. I've never liked performing. You know that, Lila."

"So you're not giving up dance?"

"Of course not." Angela finally unfolds her arms and sits down on the bottom step.

I sit next to her and say, "So you're going to keep dancing with Amala, and you're not going to perform, and you really don't care about being a professional dancer?"

"Yeah."

"I wish I could decide what I want," I say.

"You already know. You want to be a dancer. Professional. And you're good enough too," Angela says.

"I wish it were that simple. The problem is, I don't like Dana's classes. Actually, it's not that I don't like them, it's that keeping up with her class is making me give up everything else. I haven't done any homework for weeks. I practice all the time, and I still screw up."

"Maybe that's what it takes to become a professional dancer," Angela says.

"That's the problem. Is it worth it? I might have to redo English and maybe math. And I miss you and Sarit and Nini. It's not that fun at Dana's."

Angela nods and leans back against the second step. "I miss you too. It's not the same without you there."

"I could come back..."

"You mean leave Dana's studio? Isn't it what you always wanted?"

"It's everything but fun."

"You gotta have fun, Lila, or else why bother?"

"Yeah," I say. "Exactly."

I take a strand of Angela's long hair and wrap it around my wrist. We sit like that until her mom calls Angela to help her in the kitchen, and I get up to leave.

"You won't see me dancing if you're in Mexico," I say.

"I know. I'm sad about that. But I'll be swimming in the warm ocean and hanging out with Jonas and his family, so I'm not too sad."

"Have a fantastic time, Angela. I mean it."

"Thanks." Angela smiles from head to toe and gives me a huge hug.

Eighteen

"Thank goodness you're here," Eve says when I enter the change room on the morning of the festival.

"I don't think I've ever seen so much bright fabric and sparkly jewelry in one place before," I say. Every inch of the floor is covered in piles of scarves and skirts and bloomers. Girls and women have their faces plastered to the mirrors as they put on makeup and fake eyelashes and pin flowers in their hair.

Eve motions me to a corner where Alex and Robin are both half undressed. Robin waves her bra at me and says, "Help me strap myself into this thing."

"Everyone in costume in five minutes. We're doing a run-through onstage in ten," Eve says.

I've got my bra on under my hoodie, so all I have to do is pull on my skirt and make sure my hair's in place.

Robin stands in front of me, and I tie the strap of her bra tightly, then twirl around and say, "Check mine."

"It's good," she says.

We both turn to face the mirror. It's a shock to see myself. We've all covered our white bras with lace trim and sparkly sequins and have made matching belts to wrap around the long white skirts. Robin and I both have flowers in our hair and dangling earrings that sparkle in the lights.

"We look good," Robin says with surprise in her voice.

"Yeah, we do."

"Ready?" Eve says behind us. "The stage is this way."

"Where's Dana?" I ask.

"She's talking to the sound people. Now come on—we don't want to be late for the run-through." Eve shoves her way through a bunch of younger girls in silk bloomers and heads toward a door at the far end of the room.

As we follow Eve, I ask Robin and Alex, "Who died and made her God?"

"Notice she's not in costume yet," Alex says.

It's true—Eve still has a tank top on over her skirt. When we reach backstage, Eve puts her finger to her lips to indicate that we should be quiet, as if we didn't already know. Amala's troupe is onstage, running through their choreography. They're partway through already, but I step up to the curtain and watch anyway.

"They look perfect," I whisper to Robin.

"Yeah, they do."

When their music is over, they rush offstage with huge grins on their faces.

"Hi, Lila," Nini calls as she runs past.

"You were amazing," I say.

"It's going to be so much fun, but you can't see a thing with the lights on," she says.

"Lila, we're on." Eve pulls me by the arm, and I stumble after her onto the stage.

I've danced in student performances before, but never on a stage like this, with proper stage lights and cues on the floor. Nini's right. I can't see a thing except the stage itself. No way to know who is watching.

Dana's voice comes from somewhere in the audience seats. "Ready, girls? This is our final run-through before the performance. Pretend the audience is already here. Smile! Have fun!"

The music starts, but Eve calls out, "Wait. We're too far to stage right. Everyone shift three feet to the left."

We all shuffle over, and Dana's voice says, "Thank you, Eve. No stopping now. We're going to run through from beginning to end."

The music starts again. The first group of girls moves, and I count with the music. When my turn comes, I catch the timing perfectly, and the three of us swing into action. The music swells, and we head into the pinwheel. From here I can see everyone, and we're all smiling. Everything goes smoothly until the song is over, and we end.

"Come forward and bow," Dana's voice says, and we all rush to the front of the stage. "Well done, girls. We're on in half an hour, so go and finish your makeup and take a few deep breaths."

"That was great," Sam says as we head back to the change room, but Eve says, "We need to run through that shimmy sequence again," and she marches to the corner of the change room where we've left our street clothes. "Finish your makeup and come to the center of the room. We'll practice there."

"Chill, Eve," says Sam.

"Don't tell me to chill. We are going to drill for the next half hour until we walk onto that stage. We are going to be perfect." Eve's voice has an edge of frustration in it, like she's about to explode any moment.

Sam points to Eve's tank top and says, "You're not in costume."

Eve yanks off her tank top, revealing her bra underneath. "Now I am."

"Well, I want to work on my makeup, then sit quietly with my eyes closed for a few minutes before we have to go backstage," Sam says.

A voice comes over the loudspeaker. "Starting in three minutes, ladies. First two numbers backstage in one minute, please."

"You will not ruin this for me, Sam," Eve says.

Her eyes shoot sparks at Sam, but Sam shrugs and says, "I'm not ruining this for anyone, Eve."

Eve's face is red and she's having a hard time breathing, and the only thing I can think is that I want to get away from her.

"Let's go backstage and watch," Robin says.

"Good idea," I say, and the two of us creep past a few dancers and around to the backstage area. The first dance is ending as we arrive, and Amala's troupe is waiting to head on.

"Break a leg," I whisper to Sarit and Nini. Sarit hugs me. At least someone's having fun.

Amala's troupe heads onto the stage, and silence falls. I hold my breath until the music starts and the girls begin to move. *Wow, yes!* Their arms flow around them as they catch the beat of the drums, and in unison they slip into their traveling step with the violin and cello. When they twirl around to the back with the drum roll, I can see their faces shining with happiness. They turn forward again, moving to the rhythm of the accordion, and start the classic belly-dance sequence. The mirrored hip scarves dazzle in the lights, and the audience goes crazy, calling out and clapping. The energy onstage rises, and the girls dance like they're on wings, flying across the stage and smiling at each other. As the music ends, Nini whoops, and the whole troupe laughs. The clapping from the audience is thunderous, and energy and happiness radiate from the stage.

The girls grin and high-five each other as they run offstage.

"Good luck," Sarit whispers to me as she rushes past.

There's another troupe moving onto the stage, which Robin and I stay to watch, and slowly the girls from Dana's studio join us backstage. My nerves are tingling now, and when Eve steps up behind me and whispers, "Remember to count," I almost jump out of my skin.

Finally, it's our turn. We march silently onto the empty stage and form our groupings. The lights go on, and all I can see are Alex and Sam standing on either side of me. The music starts, and I count the beats of the drum. The lights are stronger than they were in the practice run, making it hard to see the girls on the other side of the stage, but it looks like they're moving flaw-lessly. When our turn comes, we catch the beat perfectly. I let out my breath and count in my head as we move through the figure eight and the shoulder motions.

"Smile," Eve whispers to Alex as she passes her, and Alex pastes a smile on her face. But then we all step into the pinwheel expertly, and I can feel the tension lessen as we move together around the stage. The oboe and oud start their conversation, and we follow the beat and the rhythm perfectly. Next comes a short section where we break into our groups again, and the movement flows across the stage in sync with the music. My hip drops radiate energy, and my undulations slide across my body. When the music changes again, we cluster in the center of the stage, and as one being we pour energy from the tips of our fingers high over our heads down through our chests, across our stomachs and hips, and into our knees. I can hear the audience roaring, but it's like the sound is coming from another room, because I'm focusing so hard on keeping my count. When the shimmy starts, and the finger cymbals crescendo, I know the song's coming to an end, and my tension falls away. We spin through to the end. I let out a huge breath. It's over.

Eve's hand grips mine as we bow, and as soon as we're behind the curtain, she pulls me into a hug. "You were perfect," she says.

"You were, Lila," says Alex.

"You too. We all were," I say.

It's true. We were all great. But as we thread our way back to the change room, I can't help sneaking glances at the girls from Amala's studio, who are sitting in a circle, laughing and sharing a bowl of taco chips. They were amazing too. Really amazing.

And they had way more fun than we did.

Nineteen

The festival is over, and there's no dance class this week so we can all catch up on our sleep and enjoy our spring break. That's what I do. Or, at least, that's what I try to do. Angela's not back for five more days, so I can't ask her for help with English, which I need to catch up on, and I don't have the energy to ask anyone else. Basically, I spend the days after the festival moping around until Mom finally says, "Lila, honey, please tell me what's going on. You've been moping for ages."

"It's nothing," I say, but she sits down at the kitchen table and pushes out a chair for me. "It's something, honey. Come on. Tell me."

"I don't know if I want to keep dancing, Mom," I say as I sit down. It feels strange to say it out loud, but it's also a relief.

"You don't want to keep dancing, or you don't want to keep dancing with Dana?"

"I don't know what I want."

Mom gets up, pulls a tray of Rice Krispies squares out of the fridge and cuts into them. She offers me one and says, "Honey, you've worked so hard on dance this term. You were absolutely amazing at the festival. You've loved to dance ever since you were about three weeks old. Okay, that's an exaggeration, but you know what I mean. Don't let one tough teacher throw you off."

I take a bite of my square and let the marshmallow melt in my mouth. "What do you think I should do?"

"I think you should go and talk to Amala. She's the one who knows your dancing best, and she's the one who gave you the opportunity to go and dance with Dana. It was always your dream, Lila. Go talk to Amala."

"Yeah. I know. I will."

* * *

Amala's studio is open, and when I peek into the room, I can see she's got a class full of women.

It must be one of her beginner classes, because she's showing them how to listen to the music by playing the beat on her drum and having them clap along. I remember doing that years ago. Belly-dance music can be really complex in its beats and rhythms and melodies, and it takes ages to learn how to listen to it properly. My hips automatically follow along as I watch, and I admire Amala's patience when some of the women miss the count and get offbeat with their clapping. Amala smiles and starts again. The class will probably last for another half hour or so. That's time enough to go over in my head what I want to say to Amala.

When the women finally come out, laughing and chatting, I stand up and wait for Amala to come to the door.

"Lila!" she says. For a second I feel bad for stopping by while she's teaching, but then she grins and says, "What a nice surprise."

"I don't want to dance with Dana anymore," I blurt out before she even has a chance to move out of the doorway.

Amala doesn't answer. Instead, she heads back into the studio and over toward the computer.

On her way, she bends and picks up a pile of scarves, which she plops into a basket at the front of the room. When she reaches the computer, she fiddles with the music for a second, then turns to me and says, "Get into position."

"Now?"

She nods and turns to start the music. I scramble from the doorway to the center of the room and strike the starting pose. Good thing I'm wearing clothes I can dance in.

The music starts. I hold the pose for eight beats, then turn slowly, snaking my arms around my body, and then, as the music gathers speed, I start the traveling step with a series of hip drops and chest lifts. With a roll of drums, I twirl. Oh, how I love this music. Next comes a series of classic belly-dance moves using hip drops and kicks, and then...suddenly I can't remember. I stumble over a few bars of music, then catch up when the music pauses for one count. It starts up again and I start with it, only to lose it again a few seconds later, and I realize that when I last danced this with Angela, in her room, I must have been following her lead, because I can't pull the choreography into my brain at all. When the music stops, I sink to the floor.

Amala heads back to the computer. "Never mind. Try this," she says, and the sound of Dana's music fills the room.

I raise an eyebrow at Amala, but she lifts her chin and starts the music again. This time I stand and get into starting position.

The music fills the room, and I dance through to the end of the song. When it's done, I say, "It's better with a full troupe because of the delayed action in some of the sections."

"And you know it like it lives inside you," Amala says.

"Yeah, I guess I do," I say.

"Dana drilled that dance into you so thoroughly you'll never forget it."

"Yeah, I guess."

"And your posture is amazing, and you're right exactly on the beat. You've learned a lot from Dana."

"I know, it's true. But..." I hesitate, because I don't really know how to put this into words.

Amala waits for me to speak, then says, "You weren't enjoying yourself."

"No." I let out a breath. "I really wasn't. And I miss Angela and Nini and Sarit. I like the girls at Dana's—especially Robin and Alex and Sam, and even Eve when she isn't being God—but it's not the same. There isn't the feeling of all of us being in it together."

Amala smiles and reaches over to hug me. "Honey, belly dance is all about being in it together. That's why I left Dana's class too. I learned so much from her, but I wanted that feeling of everyone being in it together."

"That's why I'm not sure I want to be a professional belly dancer anymore. I don't want to be like Eve." I don't tell her about the schoolwork I've not done, or the fights I've had with Angela and Nini and Sarit.

The door opens and a woman sticks her head in. "Amala, sorry, can I talk to you for one sec?"

"I'll be right back. Don't go anywhere," Amala says to me.

When she's gone, I look at all the photos on the wall. Amala takes photos at every student show and blows them up and puts them on the studio walls. There are a few new ones since I was here last, including one of Amala, mid-twirl, in a 1920s-style costume.

"That's a lovely photo of you," I say when she comes back in.

"That's from few weeks ago when I was at a festival in Seattle."

It takes my mind a second to catch up with what I'm seeing, but then it does, and I say, "Amala, you're a professional dancer. You have a great career, dancing all over the place, and you have your studio, which everyone loves, and you have fantastic classes."

"Why, thank you, Lila," she says. "Yes, I'm pretty happy with where I'm at right now. And you're right. I love the studio. It's the best part of my life, really. The best part of being a dancer is having all these lovely girls to dance with."

"But you're not like Dana," I say. "I mean, you let anyone dance with you, even if they're not fit and perfect and they don't take it super seriously. And you let the class be fun, even if everyone's not always flawlessly on time or having exact posture or doing the move correctly."

"Ouch!"

"No, I don't mean that in a bad way. The troupe was amazing at the festival. Really fantastic.

And it wasn't because their posture was perfect; it was because they loved it so much."

"Indeed." She's smiling at me like I'm a slow student who's finally getting the lesson.

"So you're telling me that there are different ways to be a dancer. Different paths to take?"

"I'm not telling you anything, Lila." She's smiling big-time now. "I chose you to go to Dana because I thought it was a good fit for you. But that's always a choice you have to make. No one can make it for you."

"So if I want to, I can come back?"

"Of course! There was never any question about that."

"It's that I don't want to feel like I'm giving up on myself. On my dream," I say. "You said a lot of Dana's students go on to have professional careers. I'm so torn, Amala, because I want that, but I also want to love dance and have fun."

"Lila, honey, you are wise beyond your years." Amala pushes a strand of hair off my face like my mother would do. "Please come back to dance with us, and bring all that you have learned from Dana with you. And later on, maybe you can dance with her again if you want to. You're going to have a great career, Lila. Especially now that you know what's important to you."

The low feeling I've been carrying around since the festival breaks open, and for the first time in days I feel like dancing.

"Do you think the other girls will have me back?"

Amala laughs. "They've been missing you so much, Lila. I'm sure they will."

"Then that's what I want to do."

The woman Amala was talking to earlier pokes her head through the door again. "Sorry, Amala, one more thing."

Amala looks at me. "We're done, aren't we?" she asks.

"Absolutely."

"Are you going to go home and tell your mom?" Amala asks as we head to the door.

"Yeah, and then tomorrow, I'm going to wait at Angela's house until she gets home from the airport and I'm going to tell her we're going to dance together again. Then—well, no. First I'm going to ask her how her trip to Mexico was."

Amala smiles and says, "Classes start again on Wednesday. See you then."

I bust out a few quick hip circles and a shoulder roll. "Yes," I say as I dance to the door. "See you then."

Acknowledgments

The best thing about writing this book was all the time I spent dancing. Here's a zaghareet for the amazing ladies at Harmony Belly Dance, especially my teacher and friend Candace Aldridge Sanchez and her family, and for Joanne Hewko, who not only didn't blush in embarrassment when I busted out dance moves on our dog walks, but danced along with me. As always, thanks to the Wildwood Writers, my family and, last but absolutely not least, my fellow writer, editor and friend Robin Stevenson.

KARI JONES loves to dance and she loves to write, so she was thrilled to have a chance to do both as she wrote *Shimmy*. Kari has written four books for children and youth, and her work has been translated into several languages. Kari lives in Victoria, British Columbia, with her husband and son. For more information, visit www.karijones.ca.

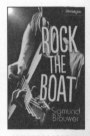

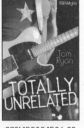